ENCOUNTERS

Best wishes

Drake Mees

DRAKE MEES

Third Edition self-published by Drake Mees through Gipping Press Ltd.

ISBN: 978-1-9161978-3-1

Print information available on the last page.

Thanks to Jenny for her painstaking work with proof-reading, Pauline and Liz, Andrew and Don making the text available on Kindle and as a paperback, Monica giving professional guidance, Jessica valuable work on translation, and for all those who encouraged me to keep going.

CONTENTS

1

HOLIDAY

David scrutinised the figures on the screen. They did not tally, but it was likely to be a small error. He pored over the columns again, and again. Then he found it. He made the alteration and punched the air in triumph. He logged off and returned papers to the filing cabinet and books to the cupboard. His desk was clear. It was a great feeling to be going on holiday. He picked up his case and lunch box and closed the office door behind him. Two weeks away from this place he thought as he walked along the corridor. There was escape, freedom, and relaxation to look forward to. He waved goodbye to Sarah in reception. She responded saying, 'Have a nice holiday,' and giving him a broad smile.

David had a few minutes walk to Charing Cross Station, then an hour on the train to Tonbridge. Once in the car he drove to the garage and filled up with diesel. Then off to the supermarket to buy sweets, plus bite-size brownies and flapjack for the journey. He knew

Emma wouldn't approve, but it was his little treat to himself.

'I'm home honey,' he announced in time-honoured fashion. 'Have you finished the packing?'

'You must be joking. I only got away from work at three o'clock. Then I had to go into town to shop.'

'Have you got some Euros?' David asked.

'Yes, that was one of the many things I had to do. Then I had to buy a few bits of food to take with us, and go to the chemists to re-stock the medical box. Since I've been home the telephone hasn't stopped ringing. First Mrs Smith, asking me what I'm making for the cake stall at tomorrow's fete. I've told her dozens of times I won't be there and I'll put twenty pounds in when I get back from holiday. Then Maureen rang and wanted to chat. She's in one of her down moods at the moment. I had to cut her off after a while with the excuse I had to go out visiting. I bet she watched to see if I really did go out. She's like that. And the cat has to be taken down the road.'

'What are you going to do for a meal?' David asked to stop his wife's 'poor me' monologue.

'I thought I would do an omelette. The bits of salad from the fridge can go with it. It won't be ready for at least an hour.'

'That's fine. It will give me time to check over the car for France. And I'll take Smudge to the cattery.' With that David was out of the house and gone.

Emma continued to carry armfuls of clothes from the wardrobe and airing cupboard and put them on the bed in the spare room. Little by little she squeezed them into the suitcases. Of course I'm looking forward to going on holiday, she thought. I need a break at the moment. I've looked forward to this for weeks, she told herself, but she knew it would be different this year. Just the two of them. No family and no lively grandchildren demanding her attention. She would miss them.

It seemed like just a few minutes had gone by when the door slammed to signal David's return. It brought her back from fond memories of recent holidays. She hurried downstairs and passed David in the hall on her way to the kitchen.

He went into the lounge and turned on the television. He plonked himself down in his favourite chair, picking up the newspaper from the coffee table as he sat down. None of the newspaper headlines grabbed his attention. The local TV news was broadcasting an item on the council's plan to reduce a play area in favour of building more sheltered housing. This didn't excite him either, in spite of the group of very vocal protestors. At least watching TV took slightly less concentration, so he drifted into this option.

Twenty minutes later Emma called him to say the meal was ready and he dutifully took his seat in the kitchen-diner.

'Wine or water?' she asked.

'I'll have water. Must have a clear head for an early start in the morning. Anyway water is good for you. Lions thrive on it, my dad used to say.'

'But that was to the children when they were young,' Emma quipped.

David changed the subject. 'What time do we check in at Folkestone tomorrow?'

'Eight o'clock.'

'Who booked us in that early, on the first morning

of the holiday?'

'I think you did. You can check whose card is on the confirmation if you like.'

He thought that was a bit unnecessary, so he continued, 'It means we need to leave by six o'clock, just in case the motorways are busy. Up before five, if we're to get everything done.'

Emma made no comment. Instead she dropped back into her reminiscences of family holidays.

'It will be different this year,' she said, stating the obvious. 'Just the two of us.'

'But it was a decision we all came to. Sue and Tom wanted to explore Norfolk. Steve and Jo wanted to go back to Cornwall. Perhaps family holidays are a thing of the past.'

'But you said you wanted to go to France and visit the Normandy beaches,' Emma reminded him. 'That was what really killed the family holiday this year. Nobody wanted to go with you! We're booked into a hotel, so you can go to the beaches during the first two days.'

David remained silent. He thought he knew why the family did not want to come with them. After the feuding and bickering between Emma and himself last year, who could blame them? And it was nearly all Emma's fault.

Emma continued her protest, 'I didn't get a choice. I have to go with you. What am I going to do while you're looking at beaches?'

'I hope you're coming with me.'

'But I'm going to be bored out of my mind. A beach is a beach, whether it's in England or Normandy.

And I don't want to look at endless miles of grave-stones.'

'I thought it would be a good time to go to Normandy, in the year of the 70th Anniversary of D-Day. I can look at the beaches where Dad and Uncle Bob came ashore. Although I guess it won't explain why dad survived the war and Uncle Bob died a few days after he landed.'

'But it's like that for me at work. Why does one person diagnosed with terminal cancer survive for six years, yet someone who looked healthier die in a matter of months? Is it just random chance, the luck of the draw? Why did the bullet that killed your uncle hit him and not somebody else? Why didn't it miss altogether?'

'This is all getting a bit deep and serious for the day before we go off on holiday,' David said. 'Why don't we clear the table and wash up, before I go out and water the plants?'

'Who's going to water them while we're away?'

'I'll give them a good soaking tonight and Jack will pop in a couple of times next week.' Further conversation stalled during the washing and wiping up.

David enjoyed the cool evening as he leisurely watered the plants. It was a welcome relief after the heat of the day and the plants were getting some much-needed moisture. If he was honest, he spent too long on the plants, but it had given him a chance to let his mind wander over what he expected from the coming holiday. OK, he hadn't thought through his plans. He would go to the beaches and visit some of the cemeteries and then what? Emma had been right to query what she was expected to do. He wasn't sure himself what was going to happen. But two days out of a week's holiday surely wouldn't be too much of a waste of time. And David did have the offer to go back to the beaches in the autumn with his friend Paul.

The light was fading fast as David put the hose away and went back into the kitchen. The smell of percolated coffee filled the room. Soon its taste washed away any lingering thoughts of his ill-planned trip to visit the D-Day beaches. It wasn't long before he and Emma climbed wearily into bed, and dropped off to sleep in an instant.

David was visited by his recurring dream of German soldiers marching through a village, their bayonets glistening in the sun, the sound of their jack-boots on the cobbles. There was the noise of distant explosions, and today the shrill sound of bells.

'I can't believe it's five o'clock already,' he grumbled, as he silenced the alarm and did his best to spring out of bed. As he made his way to the en suite, he discovered that Emma was already having a shower. Typical, he thought, and all without an alarm.

Conversation was never a big part of breakfast for Emma and David. On weekday mornings they did their own thing. Rarely were they at the table together. Even at weekends the conversation didn't sparkle. Today was one of those days when David grunted a reply to Emma or at the radio. He finished first and was about to leave the kitchen when Emma called him back.

'Can you bring the cases down and put them in the boot? I'll see to the other bits that need to go in.' He paused in the doorway to listen to Emma's request and mumbled to say he would. He then remembered there was something he needed to ask her.

'Can we check over the essential items we need to

take, after I've been round and checked doors, windows and TV? Shall we leave the answer machine on?'

'I don't see any point. We'll only come back to a string of messages from Maureen.'

After completing their individual tasks, they returned to the lounge.

'Passports? In date?' His tone resembled that of an army sergeant quizzing a subordinate, rather than a husband about to take his wife on holiday to France. Her 'Yes' to each item indicated things were as stated.

'European Health Card?' he continued. 'I've got the AA papers in my bag.'

'I've divided the Euros in two and that's yours.' Emma's tone was more gentle and conciliatory. He picked up his share of the money and put it in his wallet.

As they came out of the house, he locked the door. Once in the car, he reset the trip counter. 'We won't use Sat Nav Jane till we get to France. 05.55! Not bad,' he prided himself, as he swung his Ford Mondeo from the drive and on to the road.

There was no traffic in the village as they passed through and joined the main road. Even the M20 to Folkestone was running freely. They reached the Euro-tunnel Check-in ahead of time.

'Good morning' came the greeting from the cheery attendant. She checked their papers and gave them a letter to hang from the interior mirror. Passports were checked and they took their place in the queue to go to the train. People were running past to fetch a coffee and something to eat as if their lives depended on it.

'I'll go and get a couple of coffees,' David said, and he walked up to the café slowly and deliberately, a man who was in charge of his life and had everything under control. Why the rush, he thought, we've got plenty of time. It always seemed to him that queuing at this point took a long time, but the drive to the train was short. Then the driving on board and shuffling into position took longer. Once parked, he found his bag of delicacies and began tucking in like a school boy at his first Christmas party.

'Are you going to have some?' he asked Emma.

'I may have one, but I'm not going to pig out like you.' He ignored this barbed remark and continued to eat mini-bites and drink coffee.

'I'm now feeling fed, watered and ready for the journey, until we find somewhere for lunch,' he said.

Sat Nav Jane took them along the autoroute to Boulogne-sur-Mer and Abbeville. The roads were good, the sun shining and the traffic moderate.

'We could make Honfleur for lunch,' David suggested, after checking the clock.

'That would be nice,' Emma replied.

Honfleur had been one of their favourite stopping-off places on trips to the west coast of France. It was a mixture of old and new, old sailing ships and modern working boats. The town was always bustling with people. It was a fascinating place. Today their opportunity to enjoy its delights had to be put on hold. The péage on the Pont de Normandie wasn't able to cope with the volume of traffic, so the queue extended back some five miles along the autoroute. At last they made it into town, parked up and found a nice-looking restaurant.

He ordered a red wine to go with his steak and she ordered a white to accompany her fish. For the first time in ages they sat opposite each other, and without the distraction of television, they moved into conversation. Firstly it was about Honfleur and the people who were walking by. Then Emma changed the subject, making it more personal.

'What things do you admire about me that make you love me?' she asked.

'That's a difficult question for a man just relaxing into his lunch after a long morning on the autoroute,' he countered. 'But I'll have a go. Your friendly personality; your organised manner at work and at home; you get things done efficiently; your figure; you being a good wife to me for so many years,'

'Twenty-eight,' she said.

'I really can't imagine being married to anyone else,'

'I notice you put my figure some way down the list. And a lot of the things you mentioned are things I do, not things I am,' she insisted.

'None of us are as handsome or pretty as we were when we first met, or when we got married. You're still good looking. And you have that very pleasant friendly manner that immediately puts people at their ease.' He fumbled his way through, hoping he sounded convincing. There were aspects of Emma's character he didn't like at all, such as when she tried to put him down and when she talked behind his back.

David swirled his wine around the glass. He was looking for inspiration. 'Let me ask you the same question you asked me!' Emma was thoughtful for a while. Then she gave a measured response.

'You're smart and have a very confident manner. You seem to be in charge of your life and whatever comes your way. You're kind and generous, in time as well as money. We don't spend enough time together at the moment. That's something that needs to change.'

This last statement stopped David in his tracks. Wasn't Emma the one who was always too busy to go out? Wasn't she the one who couldn't afford the time to be with him? He put down his knife and fork before replying.

'We're both busy people, with demanding jobs that take up a lot of our time. By the end of the day I haven't much more to give.'

'But you manage to find time to play squash and golf, and meet up with your mates for a drink. And all I do is work at the Health Centre. The work there seems to spill over to life at home. Even my nights out seem to be spent with people from work. I thought love and marriage were supposed to be a bit different to this. We just seem to go on from week to week, month to month, and year to year. Don't you think we deserve better than this?'

'I do have to say that things seem to have gone downhill in the bedroom department recently. I thought that was the way things are when you get to our age!'

'So how are we going to improve things,' Emma persisted.

'I don't know,' he said, concentrating his gaze on the last pieces of food on his plate. Doing this, he could avoid eye contact. They drank the last drops of wine in silence. David waved over the waiter and paid the bill.

The walk to the car and the next part of the journey were made in uneasy silence. Emma could bear it no longer and put on a CD of classical music. It wasn't David's choice, but at least the silence had gone. When the CD finished, he upped the tempo, putting on Status Quo's Greatest Hits. He did think of playing the Rolling Stones, but thought that some of the lyrics were a bit too close to home! He turned up the volume and settled back to do battle with the traffic around Caen, which Sat Nav Jane pronounced as Cane.

It was a pleasant afternoon's drive through the Normandy countryside and it wasn't too long before they reached Port-en-Bessin. Sat Nav Jane had done her job and they found themselves outside the hotel. David got out and was given directions at reception to find the car park. Its entrance had some formidable iron gates. Emma and David took their small bags from the car and then realised it was impossible to go from the car park to their room on the same level without first going down to reception on the ground floor. Sensible, he thought.

Their room was adequate, without being lavish. Once they had unpacked, they descended by lift to reception and the bar. After the heavy conversation over lunch in Honfleur, they restricted themselves to somewhat trivial comments about the hotel and its staff.

'It's not a vast restaurant is it?'

'No, but probably sufficient for the number who will eat in. More than adequate for now!' David went and spoke to the girl at the bar.

'Would you like to order a meal, sir?'

'Yes probably. I'll have a word with my wife in a moment. I came to ask what there is to see in Port-en-Bessin.'

'It's a pity you were not here last night. There was

a street market with lots of stalls. Then fireworks. But tonight, you can enjoy walking around our beautiful town. There is sea, sand and the setting sun. There are plaques telling about how the town was set free in 1944. Also memorials to 47th Commando on the East and West Hills. The East Hill is on this side of the harbour. The memorial is above the round tower.' David thanked her for the detailed information.

'The lady at the bar is pleasant and speaks good English,' David reported back to Emma. 'I wish I could speak French as fluently.' Then he asked, 'Do we want a meal?' They agreed on salads. Again they indulged in mild chit-chat as they ate.

The day was agreeably cooler now as David and Emma set off for a stroll. They remarked how the town looked similar to many Cornish fishing villages. Fishing was the mainstay here, evidenced by the amount of tackle on the quayside and the number of buildings given over to this industry. The smell of fish was everywhere. Gulls wheeled overhead. Children were still making sandcastles on the small beach. Some people walked along the harbour wall, while others sat and stared vacantly out to sea.

David and Emma took their turn to walk around the walls at the entrance to the harbour. He was intrigued by the amount of information and old photographs describing the heroic deeds of 47th Royal Marine Commando troop. He took several photos. He then led the way scrambling up the path to the top of East Hill, where one of the memorials was situated. There were poppy wreaths on the ground and a little garden of flowers around it.

'Who looks after this?' asked Emma.

'British military, and locals who are grateful for

their freedom, I would think.' David took more photos. 'Out of 420 men, around 100 were killed, wounded or missing, in securing Port-en-Bessin for the Allies,' he said. Once back on the beach he continued his commentary. 'Down here you get a better idea of the height of the cliffs. Soldiers had to scale those to knock out the two guns at the top. Some men came from the landward side.'

Emma said nothing. She was taking in the beauty, peace and freedom that now existed on the beach. 'As you know, I hate war and everything that comes with it. I just appreciate the freedom to walk here,' she said.

The sun was setting on the water as they completed their circuit of the town. They looked at the ornaments and souvenirs of Normandy that filled the little shops crowded around the harbour. David noticed that some couples held hands, or had their arms round each other. He thought they all looked younger than him. And besides, he wasn't going to be the first to make a move and call a truce.

They made it back to the hotel in silence, each wondering what the other was thinking. David went down to reception and ordered two breakfasts for the next morning. Emma prepared some coffee. They said nothing as they drank it. David had come to Normandy to steep himself in what happened on the beaches 70 years ago. He wanted to feel part of what the Allies achieved and the events in which his father and uncle had been involved. Emma was a pacifist. She hated war and the way it had been glorified. She wanted only peace. The stage was set for an epic battle, with neither of them prepared to concede ground. This was hardly a recipe for a happy holiday, but David and Emma had decided independently they would grit their teeth during the first two days and look for better to come after that. Time would tell if their hopes would be realised.

2

BEACHES AND BATTLES

David was up early and went for a walk around the hotel. It was somewhat cooler than he expected, but the sun and clear blue sky gave the promise of a glorious day to come. Emma showered and put on what she referred to as her holiday togs. She went to the restaurant to wait for David.

They chose almost the same breakfast, from a selection of fruit juice, muesli, fresh fruit, rolls, cheese and meat, plus tea made from a bag. They ate in silence. As they were finishing, David raised a topic designed to develop or kill conversation, the weather!

'It looks as if it's going to be a good day.' Then after a pause he continued, 'I thought we'd take the D514 coast road to Ouistreham. Then we can look at Sword Beach.'

Emma didn't reply. Her body language and facial expression said it all. David realised it wasn't going to be an easy day!

'I'm happy to go along with what you want to do today and tomorrow, as we visit the beaches and the other places to do with D-Day,' he said.

'You're happy to go along with it! You're the one who's organised the trip!'

'Nothing is set in concrete,' he said, hoping to reassure Emma. 'When we get there, you can decide where you want to go. Over the next couple of days I would like to visit one or two beaches, and go to a museum and a German bunker. Then have a look at the Cemetery where Uncle Bob is buried.'

'I haven't really got a choice. The overall plan is yours, but I'll grin and bear it,' Emma said condescendingly. 'After all, it's only for two days,' she said, closing the conversation. David had intended saying that after visiting Sword Beach they could move on to Gold Beach, but he thought better of it.

Once at the car, David primed the Sat Nav and they set off for Ouistreham. It was a pleasant journey on a beautiful day. When they reached the vicinity of Ouistreham, they pulled off the road, parked up and walked to Sword Beach.

'Now this is beautiful,' said Emma, as she surveyed the shore and the waves rippling on it. 'What a pity it had to be used as a battlefield in 1944.'

'We can't change the past. We can be thankful for the outcome of the fighting, and the peace that's reigned in Europe since then.'

'Let's be thankful for the peace here today. Can we go for a walk on the beach and enjoy this place before we move on?' Emma asked.

After a break for coffee, David and Emma travelled to the Hillman Strongpoint complex of bunkers. David was intrigued to see that Hillman was situated on the Rue du Suffolk Regiment. He assumed this was in recognition of the part played by the 1st Suffolk Regiment in attacking and capturing the bunker.

'Uncle Bob was in the 1st Suffolk Regiment. Maybe he was killed somewhere here. He must be buried close by.' David's interest increased when he discovered there was a memorial and museum dedicated to the 1st Suffolk Regiment. His hopes of going on a guided tour were dashed when he found out tours only took place on Tuesday afternoons. He spent a fascinating few minutes scrambling around one of the bunkers. He was aware that Emma had moved away when he mentioned about Uncle Bob being killed. She was now a considerable distance from him. As he went to join her, he made a mental note to revisit this site.

David said, 'I'm feeling hungry! What do you say to finding a place to eat? Then we'll look for the Hermanville Cemetery?' Emma agreed reluctantly.

After their meal, Emma and David experienced different emotions as they entered the cemetery. It was much larger than any cemetery they had ever visited. The gravestones stood out in the sun, like ranks of whitened soldiers amidst the neatly cut lawns. 'This place has had an impact on me that I can't explain,' said David to break the silence. 'There's such a sense of peace and order, in contrast to the violence and bloodshed that caused these fighters to be buried here.' Emma said nothing.

There were others, like them, looking for the final resting place of relatives and friends. They moved around the gravestones with serious expressions on their faces, bending every now and then to read the inscriptions on the gravestones, then straightening up when they had once again drawn a blank.

'How will you go about looking for your Uncle Bob?' Emma asked.

'I don't know. I have no idea where he's buried. I'm not sure if we had a plot number, or the row he's buried in. All I can suggest is that we take a row each and walk quickly along it and see if we find him.'

So off they set in the blazing sun. Emma found it a tear-jerking experience, reading the ages of some soldiers as young as eighteen and nineteen when they died. She wondered what the world would have been like if these young men had grown to maturity. They continued their search for what seemed like ages. The heat sapped their energy. Suddenly, out of the blue, she stopped and shouted to David, 'I think I've found it.' He rushed over. They stood there speechless, reading the inscription.

Private
Robert Burrows
1st Suffolk Regiment
8th June 1944
Age 19

They turned so they had eye contact and hugged each other amidst a flood of tears.

'It's very strange,' David croaked. 'He died long before I was born. I know nothing about him, but he was family. He's part of me and I'm part of him. I wish dad was alive, so I could tell him I've found his brother's gravestone in Normandy.'

Emma extricated herself from David's arms and found a tissue to dab her eyes. 'As you know, I've not found today very easy,' she said, 'but I'm glad I came here. So much sorrow and suffering. Such a waste of life. It's confirmed for me why I'm a pacifist and that I should be doing more to bring peace. Everyone should be working for peace. You had better take a photo. Make a note of where the gravestone is.'

David dutifully obeyed. Then he took her hand gently in his as they walked back to the car.

'We'll go back along the coast road and I'll pull off to have a look at Arromanches. That featured in 70th Anniversary celebrations shown on television.'

'OK,' replied Emma. 'Make it quick. The experience at the cemetery has left me drained.'

It was still hot when they got out of the car and walked on the beach. Like Sword Beach it looked so picturesque, with the waves lapping on the sand. David took the opportunity to film what he could see on his digital camera.

'Look at the remains of the Mulberry Harbour,' he said pointing out to sea. 'I didn't realise there was still so much of it here.'

'What is it?'

'Parts of a temporary harbour put together to unload fuel and supplies for the beaches. There's another one at Omaha Beach, but that one got broken up by a storm. This one has lasted for seventy years.'

'I feel completely shattered, being on the go and visiting so many places,' Emma said. David was also tired and felt empathy for her. He realised his ambition to visit museums and walk on other beaches would not be achieved today. This would have to wait until another time.

'All I want now is to get back to the hotel; have a shower and cup of tea, and put my feet up,' he said.

Back in their room, David was now sufficiently re-energised to read more about the beaches and D-Day landings. He began searching through books and leaflets he had brought from home. He made notes about places he wanted to visit on his next trip.

Emma intended reading her magazine. A few lines into the first story, the magazine slipped from her grasp and she drifted off to sleep. 'I needed that. I feel so much better,' she said as she came round a long time later.

During the meal Emma was keen to pursue some of the issues which had surfaced during the day. 'Have you been able to slay some demons today?' she asked.

'I suppose so. I've been interested in D-Day since I was a kid. I got more interested when I was older and found out my father fought there and my uncle was killed. It's been one of my ambitions to go and see the beaches where the battles took place. I've seen films and TV programmes, and I wanted to go and feel part of it. I always realised if I did go, I would be duty bound to look for Uncle Bob's gravestone. The part I wasn't looking forward to was going into the cemetery. I thought it might unlock emotions that I would rather keep hidden. I never expected to find his gravestone. So the hardest part was going into that cemetery. But it was so peaceful. Then you know what happened when you found Uncle Bob's gravestone.'

'I don't think I've seen you like that before. David Burrows, financial manager, with his life sorted and organised, suddenly loses it!'

'As I said at the time, it was the realisation that part of my flesh and blood was buried in that field. So why did you shed tears?'

'The atmosphere of the cemetery had something

to do with it. Then seeing you break down, I wanted to comfort you in your sorrow.'

'That was nice. No, nice is not the right word.' He looked up at Emma. 'What about your demons?'

'Well, you know my feelings about fighting and war. I regret that D-Day ever had to take place. I've come to accept that it was necessary, if the world was to be set free from the Nazis. The various displays and memorials have brought me round to that way of thinking. But I do have to say that the story they tell is biased in favour of those on the winning side. Like you, I was dreading the cemeteries. But I found inspiration there. It would have been different if my father or uncle had died there.'

Emma continued to move the conversation forward. 'Could what happened in the cemetery be a way to give our marriage the boost that we talked about yesterday? So far we've not come up with any other ideas.'

'Perhaps,' said David. 'Maybe we can talk more about slaying our demons and repairing our marriage as we go for an after-dinner stroll.'

'I would appreciate a very short walk this evening. I still feel quite tired.'

They didn't discuss their demons or their marriage any more that day. They had a brief amble in the vicinity of the hotel. It gave Emma time to think. She knew she had discovered a chink in her husband's armour. She stored it away with other items labelled 'future exploitation'.

The next day they were suitably impressed by the Bayeux Tapestry Museum. 'The displays and explana-tions of Norman life were excellent,' David said. 'I hadn't realised it was William the Conqueror who set up our monetary system of pounds, shillings and pence nearly a thousand years ago.'

They found the tapestry itself just as impressive. 'Much longer than I had imagined,' Emma said. 'We've known about this since we were kids, and we've seen photos of it, but it's even better when you see it in real life, don't you think? I think it's brilliant.'

As they came out of the museum, Emma said, 'I'm ready for a coffee.' She led David to a suitably named café a short walk away.

They made a perfunctory visit to the Battle of Normandy Museum. Then they crossed the road for a brief look at the British Commonwealth Cemetery, which was much larger than Hermanville and contained over 4,500 burials. Emma and David restricted themselves to reading the inscriptions on the main memorials and then walking along a few ranks of gravestones. They remarked on the large number of regiments represented and came across gravestones for soldiers, sailors and airmen from many countries, including Poland, Germany, Australia and Canada.

As they walked towards the exit, Emma said, 'Is that it? Have you seen enough?'

By now David had found it difficult to maintain his enthusiasm after making so many visits. 'I'm ready to move on. I will have to leave anything else for another time.'

'Are you saying that we can now enjoy the rest of our holiday?' she asked very pointedly.

'I suppose I am, if you put it like that!'

'I don't want to see another beach, museum or cemetery during the rest of this week,' she said with a smirk. 'We can have lunch in Carentan. Then I'll need to do some food shopping before we go to the gîte,' she added.

When they arrived back at the car, David prepared the Sat Nav. 'I'll put in Carentan and follow the directions. I'm sure you would be able to get us there just as well as the Sat Nav,' he said with a smile.

As they set off, David admitted to feeling hungry. 'It shouldn't take us long to get to Carentan,' he said. As they travelled the country roads, Emma relaxed more into holiday mode. She felt that the beaches and battlefields were consigned to the past and not to be visited by her again.

The Sat Nav gave the instruction, 'Go right on the roundabout, second exit.' David obeyed. As he was passing the first exit, a big, black car came from nowhere and struck the front wing of his car, forcing him on to the roundabout.

'What the ….?' David let out. The other vehicle took the exit he was aiming for and was gone. 'Try and remember any details. I'll stop when I can,' he said to Emma.

3

FIND THAT CAR

When he found a suitable place, David pulled his car off the road and inspected it. He said to Emma, 'He's put a dent in the right wing. At least the car's still driveable. I'll have to give my insurers a call later. Now, what can we remember about the other car?'

'A black BMW with dark windows.'

'Registration starting with B,' added David

'B space MM,' Emma confirmed. 'And it was registered in Germany.'

'Did we get any sight of the driver?'

'No, none at all. I didn't even see what type of BMW it was. It all happened so quickly!'

'There's only a remote chance of seeing the car again,' David said. 'But we need to be on the look out for it.'

Minutes later they arrived in Carentan. David drove into a large, central car park. 'Food first, every-thing else later,' he said. He locked the car and surveyed the damage once more, running his hand over the dent. He then caught up with Emma as she walked towards the main street. A café at the far end looked good and they opted to eat outside, as it was still hot. The waiter brought them drinks and there was time to ponder the accident before the food arrived.

'At least neither of us was injured,' said David. 'There is minor damage to my car. Hopefully that can be repaired without costing too much. I do feel a bit shaken up though. It's as if someone invaded my space. Rather like being burgled.'

Emma said, 'I could see this black car coming very quickly to the roundabout. I thought I hope he stops. I didn't think for one minute he would hit us.'

'I just wonder what he was thinking about,' said David. 'Was he distracted? Or was he just going too fast?'

'We'll probably never know.' said Emma. 'As you said, it's unlikely we'll see that BMW again.'

After a pleasant lunch, David said he would give his insurance company a ring and Emma went off to do some shopping.

'Do be on the look out for that car,' he called after her.

The phone call to the insurance company was not easy. The agent took down David's details. He asked him about the damage to his Mondeo. Having found out this was minimal and the car was still driveable, he went on to ask for details about the accident. David told him what happened.

'Do you have a description of the other vehicle?'

'It was a large, black BMW with German licence plates. It had a B followed by MM and then some numbers. My wife and I didn't manage to see the numbers. The car hit my Mondeo and pushed me on to the roundabout. It then sped off at the next exit, before I had time to work out what had happened.' As he said this, David felt his answer lacked important details.

'It would be helpful if you would write down all you can remember about the accident, Mr Burrows,' the agent said. 'I will put some forms in the post, so you can provide us with this information, plus any sketches to show the position of the vehicles at the point of impact. I will also send details of the body shop to which you can take your car when you get back to England.' Having ascertained how long David would be on holiday in France, he said, 'All the papers should be waiting for you by the time you arrive home.' David thanked him and rang off.

Emma will be awhile shopping, he thought, so I might as well explore Carentan. So this was the centre of the German defence strategy against the Allied offensive in June 1944. It's been rebuilt and looks good.

As David walked across the car park, he glimpsed a large black car in the far corner. His heart skipped a beat! As he got closer, he noticed damage to the paintwork on the driver's side and it was a BMW, registered in Germany. The licence plates had the letter B, then two coloured circles and MM, followed by 3685. He took out his camera and removed the cover. Then holding the camera at waist level, he took what he hoped would be photos of the licence plates and the damage to the front wing. He pocketed his camera and walked nonchalantly away. As he did so, he realised he was being approached by a smartly-dressed lady with dark, shoulder-length hair, whom he guessed was in her forties.

'Why did you take photos of that car?' she asked.

David went on the offensive. After all, he was the one against whom a crime had been committed earlier. 'That car nearly took me off the road on my way to Carentan. It damaged my front wing. Is this your car?'

'No.'

'Were you driving it?'

'No.'

'Do you know who owns the car?'

The pause before she answered indicated to David that she did indeed know who owned the vehicle.

'I do not own the car,' she said.

David was left to wonder how he could continue the conversation from here. He pondered the facts he knew - that he was speaking with a lady who knew more about the ownership of the BMW than she was prepared to reveal. The car had German licence plates, so she was perhaps German. Yet she was speaking to him in eloquent English, without any sign of an accent.

'Do you work for the German government?'

'No.'

'So what brings you here?'

'I could ask you the same question! I think I know what the answer will be, that you are on holiday.'

'Yes. And are you on holiday?'

'Yes, in a way.'

David felt he had lost ground. He should be the one calling the shots. He should put her under scrutiny, so he asked, 'What is your name?'

'My name is Anna.'

'I'm David,' he replied. 'And would I be right to think you live in Germany?'

'Yes, I do. Where do you live in England?'

There she goes again, he thought, trying to steal the high ground. He side-stepped the question and summarised the situation as far as he understood it. 'This car, which you don't own and you weren't driving, hit my Mondeo on a roundabout earlier today. It then sped off without stopping.' David thought he had done well and Anna didn't refute what he said. He continued, 'I have been in touch with my insurers. They have asked me to send in a report of the collision, together with details of the other vehicle, this vehicle, which I now have. I also have photographic evidence, showing damage to the BMW.' David felt he had now regained the upper hand. He went on,

'My insurers will then contact the owner, or the owner's insurance company, to claim back the cost of repairing my car.'

David congratulated himself on putting his case so clearly and concisely. However, he was not prepared for Anna's reply. Smiling sweetly she said, 'There will be no problem with payment!'

'And how do I obtain that payment?' David asked quizzically.

'I will get it to you. Are you on holiday in this area for this week?'

David nodded with a grunt and then added, 'My car won't be repaired until I get home. I won't know the cost till then.' He spoke rather hesitatingly. The bottom line was that he didn't want to give away too many details of his holiday to a complete stranger, who was also linked to the black BMW which had hit him. He wondered what he was committing himself to.

'I have to be in La Haye-du-Puits tomorrow

afternoon. You could meet me there. I will give you an address, to which the invoice for the repair of your Mondeo should be sent. There are a number of places in La Haye-du-Puits where we can have a drink.'

'But how will I know which café you are in?' David asked.

'In weather like this I will be sitting outside, waiting for you to buy me a coffee! I will see you tomorrow afternoon at three o'clock.' She adjusted the bag on her shoulder and walked quickly away, her dark hair trailing behind her. David was bewildered. He wouldn't have known what to say if Anna was still there in front of him. I had better go and see if Emma has finished shopping, he thought.

David arrived at the supermarket just as Emma was emerging, her arms laden with bags. 'Good timing, I reckon,' he said, bristling with pride.

'It would have been, if you had arrived five or ten minutes ago. Then you could have helped me with the bagging up.' He took a share of the bags from Emma and they walked to the car in silence. This was not the time to tell her about Anna.

There was little traffic and the journey to the gîte was uneventful. Neither of them ventured to break the silence. Emma felt David had let her down. She thought he had spent time on goodness knows what, when he should have been in the shop with her. David realised he had messed up. It wasn't the best start to getting their marriage back on track. He noticed the road went through La Haye-du-Puits on the way to Bretteville-sur-Ay on the coast. When they arrived at the gîte, David suggested he should empty the car and take the shopping to the kitchen, while Emma prepared a meal.

'Would you like a cup of tea or coffee, or a glass of wine,' he asked.

'Wine would be good,' was Emma's curt reply.

During the meal David had the opportunity to tell Emma what had happened in the afternoon, while she was shopping. 'I gave my insurance company a call. I was told to continue using the car carefully, as there was only minor damage to the front wing. There will be forms I have to complete about the accident waiting for us when we get home. One of them asks for full details of the vehicle that hit us.'

'Which we don't have,' Emma said quickly.

'Yes, but wait!' David was going to enjoy telling his story to Emma. 'As I walked around Carentan, in the corner of the car park I could see a large BMW. It had German plates with B then MM and 3685.'

Emma's interest was aroused. 'But how do we know who it belongs to? And how do you get the money for the repair of your car?'

'I'm coming to that.' David realised Emma was keen to hear more. 'As I walked away from the car, I was approached by a young lady called Anna. She asked me why I had taken photos of the car. As we talked, I found out she was German, but spoke English as well as we do. She is not the owner of the BMW. Nor was she driving when the accident happened. But she said there would be no problem paying for my car to be repaired.'

'How?'

'I'm meeting Anna in a café in La Haye-du-Puits tomorrow afternoon. She will give me details of where to send the repair invoice. She was charming and seemed thoroughly honest.'

'I might have known! David Burrows up to his old tricks again! You're a sucker for any vaguely attractive female. How do you know she'll turn up tomorrow? How do you know she'll give you any address to send the invoice to? Once we're back in England that will be it. You may have an address, but I don't think you'll get any money. This all seems a bit far-fetched. I reckon this Anna thought she should challenge you when she saw you taking photos of the car. When she realised it was your car the BMW hit, she made up some story about paying your repair costs.'

'If nothing happens, I'm wrong and you're right. Then I'll have to sort it out with my insurers.'

'I think you need to be very careful. I don't want to sound melodramatic, but this sounds a bit like some sort of spy story. Who was driving the BMW? Where will the money come from to pay for the repair? Did she say what she said, just to shut you up? It may be better to have nothing to do with this Anna. You can afford to pay for the repair and then you'll avoid meeting up with her again, especially if she is pretty.'

David got up and started to clear the table. That hadn't gone as well as he had hoped. 'Where do you want to go tomorrow?' he asked. 'I managed to put together an itinerary for the first couple of days. Did you ever find anything worth visiting on the Cherbourg Peninsula?'

'Of course I didn't,' Emma snapped. 'I was too busy before we came away, or hadn't you noticed?' She was now getting really wound up. 'It's not where do I want to go tomorrow, but since you've met this Anna, it's where do I want to go tomorrow morning. First it was beaches, museums and cemeteries. Now on the first day of our real holiday it's morning only. Just so you can go and meet her in the afternoon.'

David felt he had no answer to this onslaught, so he said nothing. While Emma curled up on the sofa with her book, he busied himself looking through the leaflets on the coffee table. This didn't keep his interest for long. His thoughts soon turned to Anna. She is attractive, he thought, and she does have a lovely personality. I can't wait to see her again tomorrow.

4

STRANGE BUT TRUE

Early the next day, David re-visited his dream about German soldiers with gleaming bayonets. This time they were not marching, but strung out across the street to form a human barricade, defying anyone to cross. He thought he was in a small town in Normandy. Suddenly there was the loud noise of a tractor, which woke him up.

'What's going on? What are they doing?' he shouted. He jumped out of bed, rushed across the bedroom and flung open the curtains. A tractor pulling a trailer was weaving its way along the track between the gîtes. The driver was out of David's view. But amongst the bins, buckets, pots and nets on the trailer, there was a man wearing a bright orange hat. He was being jolted from side to side as the trailer wheels went into potholes along the way. 'What are they doing?' David repeated. 'Don't they know it's only seven o'clock in the morning?'

'Perhaps it's the time they go to work,' said Emma. 'Anyway, now you're up, you can go downstairs and make a cup of tea.' David grabbed his dressing gown and set off like a chastened child.

Later David had a shower and helped himself to breakfast. Then he picked up two of the leaflets and went out to the car. It was already hot and it was only eight o'clock. He opened the windows, so he could feel the breeze drifting through the car. As he read one of the leaflets, he was aware of an engine noise getting louder, as a vehicle approached. Suddenly it was much louder, as it passed by, on the other side of the garden fence. It was the tractor! He jumped out of the Mondeo, not bothering to shut the door. He ran through the kitchen, up the stairs and into the bedroom. Emma was in the final stages of putting on make-up when David burst into the room.

'It's the tractor,' he shouted, like a schoolboy seeing one for the first time. Orange hat was driving the tractor. A larger, older man, wearing jeans and a dirty T-shirt, was slumped amongst the fishing equipment on the trailer.

The tractor stopped behind a tall, white van and the trailer was backed up to it. Driver and passenger jumped down and mysteriously, a third man appeared, wearing a fishing apron and a black baseball cap. The other two donned fishing aprons. Then all three began emptying buckets and bins from the trailer into the white van. Pieces of fishing tackle were put into a large shipping container. David was intrigued to see what appeared to be a play being acted out on the other side of the fence.

When the trailer was empty, the man with the dirty T-shirt went and picked up a hose. The other two placed empty buckets and bins, crab and lobster pots on an area of concrete and the third man hosed them down.

The others assisted with the cleaning, by scrubbing the items using large brooms. Once the cleaning was finished, all the clean items were put into the container. The water on the concrete was vigorously swept on to the surrounding grass. The man with the baseball cap swung the van doors closed and pulled down the locking lever. He then got into the driving seat and set off along the bumpy track. The other two disappeared into a brick building nearby.

'I'd like to know if they're French or some other nationality,' said David, realising Emma was still in the room. She had watched the final stages of the drama. 'That was all completed in less than half an hour,' he observed. 'I wonder why everything has to be done in such a rush.'

'Perhaps there's a deadline to get the catch to market,' said Emma, who was now ready to meet the world. 'What have you planned for today, sorry, this morning?' she asked.

'I was thinking about that when the tractor returned,' David said. 'I can show you in the atlas in the car.' They picked up a few bits and pieces, locked up and got into the Mondeo.

David showed Emma on the map. 'I thought we could go north on the coast road from Bretteville-sur-Ay. Then join the D650 and drive up to les Pieux. We can stop if there's a great view and when we need coffee and lunch. It will have to be an early lunch, so I can get back to meet Anna in La Haye-du-Puits this afternoon.'

'I had almost forgotten about Anna,' Emma said sarcastically. She said no more, not wanting to be accused of being more bitchy than she had already been. Conversation throughout the morning and during coffee and lunch was brief and polite. No more, no less.

David dropped Emma off at the gîte, turned the car around and set off for La Haye-du-Puits. As he drove into the town, he noticed a car park sign. He followed it and came into a large parking area. There were few cars in the upper part. He drove through to the bottom end. He hadn't seen the BMW. Perhaps Anna isn't here, he thought. Perhaps she isn't coming. Or perhaps she's used another car park.

He knew nothing about the town. He walked towards what he assumed was the centre. Then he took a main street, which was full of shops, restaurants and bars. At least this area was bustling with people. As he continued along the street, he noticed someone in the distance, sitting at a street café. Now that's where she ought to be sitting, to make it easy for me to see her, he thought. As he got nearer, he realised it was her.

'Hello, Anna,' he said.

'Hello, David,' she replied. 'It is good to see you again.'

'I hope you haven't been waiting long.'

'Only a few minutes.' He sat down and soon a waiter came over and took their order.

'I remember you are paying,' she said with a smile. 'I have brought you this,' she went on, taking an envelope from her handbag. On the front was written David, in small, neat handwriting. 'You can open it.' He did so and took out a piece of paper folded in half. When he unfolded it there was an address:

Mustermann
Postfach 21223
70563 Stuttgart
Germany

Two coffees arrived, but David hardly noticed. He was too engrossed with the address on the paper.

'Mustermann, is that you?' he enquired politely.

'No, it is the family I live with,' she replied.

'Live with? Don't you live with your own family?'

'Not any more.'

'So who is Mustermann?'

'It is the family name of the people who took me in many years ago.'

'When you were a child?'

'When I was older, a young person.'

'So where do you live?'

'In a castle built on the side of a mountain some distance above Stuttgart.'

'And how many people live in the castle?'

'Two adults. I think you would call them foster parents in England. And their son, Franz.'

'Your husband or boyfriend?'

'No, my minder! He is much younger than me.'

'Minder, eh? So what does that involve?'

'He takes care of me. He makes sure I come to no harm.'

'So where is he now? He doesn't seem to be looking after you at the moment!'

'He has other things to do, business interests to look after.'

'In Normandy?'

'Yes, in Normandy.'

'So it's the Mustermann family who will pay for the repair of my car?'

'Yes.'

'And was it Franz who was driving the BMW yesterday, when it hit my car?'

Anna hesitated, and then said, 'Yes, it was. He is only in his early twenties, and he drives too fast. He is a great fan of Michael Schumacher! He goes too quickly towards roundabouts, whether or not there are other cars on the road. You happened to be on the roundabout yesterday, so he hit you! It could not be avoided.'

'But the family is prepared to pay for his bad driving?'

She smiled and said, 'Yes. They have done it before and they will do so again. It is all part of him being the son and active partner in the business. He takes a salary and expenses.'

'I see now why you were so confident that the cost of the repair to my car would be paid. They must be a wealthy family, and they must be in a very good business. What sort of business is it?'

'I cannot tell you any more. I have probably said too much already.'

David leaned back in his chair and drained his cup. 'Will you have another?' he asked.

'I had better not. I need to be picked up soon,' she added, looking at her watch. 'And you are on holiday with your wife; you need to spend time with her.'

David fell silent. Then he said, 'But I would like to see you again. To find out more about you. To discover how you come to be living with the Mustermann family.'

'And you like to be in the company of a beautiful woman!' she added. This almost made him blush.

'How about meeting me tomorrow at the same

time?' she asked.

'That would be a bit too soon,' he replied. 'Perhaps on Thursday afternoon, same time, same place?'

'OK then,' Anna said, as she got to her feet and picked up her handbag. She was about to walk away, when she turned back to David and said, 'I will see you around three o'clock in two days time. And remember, you are paying for the coffee!'

David called over the waiter and paid the bill. As he walked slowly back to his car, he felt a warm glow all over. It was not just because of the hot weather. Once in the car, he paused to think about the things Anna had told him. What was it Emma had said last night? 'I think you should be very careful.' She then talked about a spy story she had heard about and advised him to have nothing more to do with Anna. But I'm intrigued and she is rather attractive, he thought. Then after a long pause, he said out loud, 'What am I going to tell Emma?'

David drove slowly back to the gîte, trying to recall snippets of his discussion with Anna. He felt the adrenaline causing his heart to pound. He must drive on the right and be very careful.

As soon as he walked through the door, Emma went on the offensive.

'Did she come up to your expectations?'

David ignored her innuendo. 'She was there. She gave me an envelope containing a piece of paper. On it was the address to which I have to send the invoice for my car repair. The family she lives with…'

'She's not married then?' Emma interrupted.

'The family lives in a castle near Stuttgart. The

address is their PO Box number. They are called Mustermann and they are in business.'

'What sort of business?'

'Anna wouldn't say. I have every reason to believe that she's telling the truth. She seems very genuine and honest. The business is run by the father and his son and I'm sure it can afford to pay for the repair of my car. The son's name is Franz, he's in his 20's. He is Anna's minder. I'm not exactly sure what that means.'

'We might make an educated guess!' Emma said.

'The son, Franz, drives like an idiot. He was driving the BMW yesterday. This wasn't his first accident. My repair costs will come out of his business expenses.'

Emma was silent for a while. She was re-loading rounds for her next volley. Then after each one was fired, she paused, for greater effect.

'I still think you need to be careful. I have great concerns over this so-called business. Anna may be the bait to lure you into some financial scam. You need to mind what you say. And think about what you do. And watch your back.' Then Emma dropped the final bombshell, 'You haven't arranged to see her again, have you?'

This caught David somewhat off guard. 'I said I would see her on Thursday. She has an amazing story. I've only heard little bits of it so far.'

'How do you know that? This meeting up again has nothing to do with the fact that she is an attractive young lady, I don't suppose?'

David picked up a glass and poured himself some water from the tap. He drank deeply. Then he sank into an armchair and slowly finished the rest. 'I thought we were trying to get our marriage back on track,' he said.

'But I don't think that will be helped by you meeting up with another woman, just when you want to,' Emma said.

David pressed on, 'I thought we might go for a walk on the beach after we've had a meal. Then we can talk. What do you think?'

By this time Emma was busy collecting things together for a meal. She refused to be drawn on his suggestion and made no reply.

As they walked along the beach in silence, they both realised there was a huge rift between them. Their faces reflected what was going on in their hearts. David realised that on this occasion he was largely to blame. At a time when he and Emma were trying to find some common ground on which to re-build their marriage, he had invited another joker to join the game. Anna might indeed become the knave of hearts.

Emma was walking by the water's edge and at a slower pace than David. Her mind was in turmoil. Her heart felt shattered. She felt she'd been betrayed. She had not wanted to do the D-Day bit, but that had gone reasonably well. Since then, things had gone downhill fast. He was the one who had caused this by bringing another woman into the holiday. Emma felt she had to be strong and do what she could to save her marriage. After all, that was what she and David longed for. She must stand up for what she believed in, even if it meant removing cocky Mr David Burrows from his perch once in a while!

David was still a great distance along the beach from the fishermen. He knew they wouldn't walk that far this evening. He was about to tell Emma about his idea to walk right up to the fishermen some other time. When he looked round, he discovered she was far away from him and walking in the other direction.

5

TRIVIAL PURSUITS

David sat up in bed and exclaimed, 'That tractor's as good as an alarm clock.' He slid out of
bed and made his way to the window. Once
again the tractor and trailer bumped their way along
the lane, waking people as they went. Today there was
a new man with yellow waders being shaken on board
the trailer. It was not long before the tractor disappeared
from view. David made a mental note to be back at the
window by eight o'clock. He wanted a grandstand view
of today's action.

Almost on time, the tractor and trailer returned.
Again three characters acted out the same play as
yesterday. Crabs and lobsters were packed into crates
and put into the white van, together with bins that
David thought may have contained shellfish. The
hosing down ritual then followed. The van doors were
locked and the well-built man drove off along the
bumpy track, leaving the other two to exit stage left and
go into the shed.

There must be more to this than meets the eye,

David thought. If we go for a walk this evening, I would like to get a closer look at the fishing boat and its equipment. After the experience of last night, he was not optimistic about another walk though. As he came down the stairs Emma was standing in the middle of the kitchen, sipping coffee.

'I thought we might go to Cherbourg today and explore some of the north-west coast too,' David ventured.

'I had the same idea,' Emma replied. 'Having read some of the leaflets, it looks to be a place worth visiting. It must be an omen, us agreeing over something, after the last few days of fighting,' she said, with a touch of humour. Perhaps she was seeing the need for them to change, David thought. He would reserve judgement till the end of the day. At least the signs were good at the moment.

They shared in some light-hearted conversation during the day. They avoided speaking about Anna, or D-Day, or their marriage. On the way back Emma said she would need to go into town to shop for food. David made his way to La Haye-du-puits, which he had visited yesterday. There were enough shops for Emma to buy food, he thought.

As David drove the Mondeo into the car park, they both caught sight of a large black BMW parked near the entrance. Neither said anything. David's first glance told him it was not the car. There was no damage to the front wing. A second look enabled him to recognise the familiar registration plate. He drove around the car park and found a parking place well away from the BMW and other cars.

'You won't be long will you?' he said. 'I'll wait in the car.' He made it sound as though he was doing

Emma a favour by not going shopping! He needed to be in a position where he had a clear view of the BMW. He dare not go anywhere near it. He could not be sure if the driver was Anna or Franz. He lowered the two front windows. That allowed a pleasant breeze into the car. He waited and waited, but there was no sign of a driver for the BMW. As time went by, he calculated that there was a greater chance of Emma returning before, or at the same time, as the BMW driver. If that was Anna, it could be a disaster. What should he do? As he was thinking this through, there was a tap on the roof of his car.

'Hello, David,' said Anna. 'I did not expect to see you here.' Once again she had gained the advantage. He was like a young boy caught with his hand in a jar of sweets.

'No, I didn't expect to see you either,' he replied. He opened his door and started to get out.

'Franz has put quite a dent in your car,' Anna remarked. She's a clever cookie to notice that, he thought.

'I see your car has been repaired,' he said.

'Yes, Franz has organised that.'

He had now extricated himself from his car, but things could still be difficult. If Emma arrived back and saw him talking to Anna, he didn't know what he would do. He locked the car with the remote and started to hurry off across the car park.

'I'm just going to look for my wife. She's gone shopping,' he called back to Anna.

'You are still OK for tomorrow?' she enquired.

'Yes, yes,' he said more quickly.

As he hurried on, he was unsure if he had closed

the car windows. He was not going back to check. If he did, he might meet Anna again.

David met Emma on the main street. He offered to carry her only bag. 'That's alright, I can manage,' Emma replied. 'I thought you were going to put your feet up and wait for me in the car.' David didn't answer. 'I've got some sausages and burgers. I thought we could have a barbecue. There's everything you need at the gîte. If you do the cooking, I'll prepare the rest of the food in the kitchen,' she said.

David's heart sank. His mind went back to the previous summer, when Emma had invited a number of her friends round for a barbecue on a particularly hot day. As the guests started arriving, it clouded over and started to rain. Eventually it turned into a fully-fledged thunderstorm. David was the only one left outside, still trying to cook the food. Finally he had to admit defeat. He had taken the food into the kitchen, to be finished in the oven. Emma had said he had shown her up in front of her friends. She vowed she would not invite them again. Was she now trying to remind him of his failure? Although there seemed to be no sign of rain in Normandy today, he was not looking forward to doing battle with an unknown barbecue. He therefore gave a muted reply to Emma's suggestion.

As they walked past a patisserie, Emma remarked that the fruit tarts in the window looked delicious.

'Well go in and get one large or two small ones and that will do for dessert,' David said.

By the time they arrived back at the car park the BMW had gone. David felt more confident now to talk about it.

'Did you see a BMW when we drove into the car park?' he asked.

'I noticed a black BMW, but I wasn't sure if that was the one.'

'It was. I could tell from the licence plates. When I looked closer I could see that the damage to its front had been repaired.' He wondered if he had said too much in making this last remark. He said no more and Emma didn't pick up on it.

The barbecue was remarkably easy to light with the firelighters provided with the charcoal. It was not long before there were enough glowing embers over which to cook the sausages and burgers. There was only one flaw in an otherwise faultless performance. One sausage had a mind of its own. It did a flip from the griddle into the fire and it was cremated in the ensuing flames. On this occasion Emma did not berate her husband, as she was accustomed to do.

'It's been a good day, David said. 'Your idea of having a barbecue was excellent. All washed down with some splendid wine, and finished off with those lovely tarts.' He deliberately didn't look at Emma when he said these closing words. He thought she might be looking disapprovingly at him.

As they walked along the beach, they managed to start talking about ways to improve their marriage. David was surprised at the openness Emma was showing. She was certainly displaying a different side to her character compared to her attitude on previous days. One of the key suggestions was to spend more time together, sacrificing time, spent on other things, for each other. They agreed to put this into practice as soon as they got home, as a matter of some urgency.

'Last night when we were here,' David said, 'I suddenly remembered something I wanted to say to you. When I turned round, you were walking back along the beach.'

'I know. I was so tired,' Emma replied. David was unable to detect any hint of apology in her voice. 'I will try to do better tonight,' she added.

They walked at a leisurely pace along the wet sand. The air was still warm, so the sea breeze was welcome. David thought he should tell Emma his plan to get closer to the fishing boats. 'You see those boats, maybe a mile or so away. I want to get near enough to see if there's anything other than crabs and lobsters in those pots,' he said.

'Such as?' Emma replied.

'Drugs,' David suggested.

'You're always suspicious of people doing a perfectly ordinary job, like fishing for crabs and lobsters, doing something illegal.'

'But the Channel Islands are not that far away, or they could rendezvous with a boat in the Channel.'

Emma didn't want to prolong the argument, but she did warn David to be careful.

As they got closer, they could see the concrete jetty running from the top of the beach to the water's edge. The tractor had done its job, dragging the boats to the sea. It was now nowhere to be seen.

'I assume that is where the tractor and trailer come to each morning,' David said. 'Leave base at seven o'clock. Travel down here and load the catch. Back by eight o'clock.' Emma didn't say a word. Although his description seemed plausible, she didn't want to encourage him by saying she agreed.

'We're not going to get near enough tonight,' David said. 'We need to be here earlier tomorrow.' As far as he could see, there appeared to be two men in each fishing boat. Other fishermen wearing waders manoeuvred the boats into the sea. Once there, outboards sprang to life. The boats were off, circling across the water on their pre-ordained journeys.

'That's all I need to see,' said David, taking Emma's hand. Her grip was gentle, but firm. He thought perhaps this was the start of the better relationship for which they both longed. The sincere words they had spoken earlier had now turned into action. There was no need to speak. Holding hands said it all.

Over coffee back at the gîte, Emma offered a suggestion about what they might do the next day. 'I would like to go to the Mont-Saint-Michel. Do you know how far it is?'

'I can work it out from the atlas,' David said. After a while, he added, 'Around 100 miles. Two hours or so to get there.'

'I do realise,' said Emma, 'that we will have to leave after an early lunch, if you're to get back in time to meet that woman in the afternoon.' She was making a factual statement and not trying to be bitchy. David remained silent. Emma went up to bed. David browsed the leaflets about the Mont-Saint-Michel. He wanted to make the most of the time they would have there, especially as it was only half a day.

The next morning the sun shone as bright as ever. The tractor and trailer once again left around seven o'clock and returned with the night's catch about an hour later. David was already getting used to the routine after only two days. Today there were no new characters. The work schedule was the same as before. Once the van doors were locked, it was driven away, today by orange hat. The older man was there, but when the work was finished, he went into the shed. David wondered if this was promotion for orange hat, but realised he would never know.

The trip to the Mont-Saint-Michel took just over two hours, as David had predicted. The nearer they got, the heavier the traffic became. David was fortunate to find a space in the crowded car park so quickly. Then it was off for coffee and sightseeing.

'We've had some fantastic weather this week,' said Emma as she drank her coffee. 'I could get used to this lifestyle any day.'

David was in a sombre mood. He was thinking deeply. Was it about what he thought might be going on behind the fishing operations at Bretteville-sur-Ay? Or was it about Anna? He did wonder how he would find out more about her when they met later that day. He then broke the present silence by suggesting he and Emma should go on a tour of the Abbey.

'Good that,' he exclaimed, 'only two English tours a day, and when we arrive, there's room on the morning one!'

'What an enchanting place,' Emma said, as they came to the end of the tour. 'What history! What views! You get the feeling of what it must have been like for the early monks. I'm glad I wasn't one of them.'

'No chance of that,' David teased. Then after a pause he said, 'I've taken some photos. I'd like a few more from sea-level. Then I'm suggesting we eat. I can take photos as we walk.'

All the restaurants were crowded, but they did manage to find an empty table for two. They both ordered omelettes. 'I read that over 4 million people visit the Mont-Saint-Michel every year,' said Emma.

'A lot of them today,' David added. People had come by coach and car. Some were on the grand tour from China, Japan, France, Europe, UK and US. 'I have to admit it's a wonderful place,' he went on. 'It has a special atmosphere. Now we've had lunch, we had best be on our way back.'

It was an uneventful journey. Emma fell asleep early on. David put on a Bee Gees CD and kept the volume low. Emma woke up as the car bumped and lurched along the lane to the gîte. David dropped her off, turned the car round and set off for La Haye-du-puits. Although it had been a great experience to see the Mont-Saint-Michel and the lunch was good, he was looking forward to this afternoon more than anything.

He parked in the usual car park and made straight for the café. There was no sign of Anna. He sat down and waited. When the waitress asked for his order, he explained that he would order when his friend arrived. As he waited, David tried to think through how he could find out more about Anna. He didn't want to bombard her with so many questions that he frightened her away. On the other hand, he wanted to discover more of her interesting story and he would only do that by asking questions. Eventually Anna made it, some twenty minutes late.

'I'm sorry I'm late,' Anna said.

'That's OK,' he reassured her.

Having completed the formality of ordering coffee, David got straight to the point. 'I know something about the family you live with, but I know very little about you. Tell me about your background and your childhood.'

Anna smiled and took a sip of coffee. David had offered her the stage and she was more than willing to take it. 'Have you heard of the Baader-Meinhof gang?' Her opening words came as a big shock. Perhaps he was expecting to hear about a little girl who was saved from the streets of some German city, to be looked after by a rich family. He nodded and said a muffled, 'Yes.'

'The group started from a radical student movement in the late 1960's. They were mainly middle class young people. They were fighting against the West German capitalist system. They killed prominent industrialists and business men. Many young people were sympathetic to their aims and some joined them. The gang became like a family, bound together by the same ideology.' Anna paused for another drink.

David could hear Emma's words ringing in his mind. However, he was intrigued to find out how Anna had been involved with this gang. She continued, 'As time went by children were born. They were moved around from house to house, so the whereabouts of gang members would not be compromised. There were many sympathisers.'

He could wait no longer, 'So how did you come to be involved?'

Anna had her own script. She would answer his question as the story unfolded. 'Some of the older children left West Germany and were moved across Europe. They ended up in Sicily. I was younger. I didn't go to Sicily until I was, as you would say, a teenager. By then all the older children had left. It was a great place to be. Sun and sand. I had a few lessons, mainly learning languages.'

'How many do you speak?' David asked.

'Five. German of course, French, English, Italian, and Spanish.'

David felt he had to go on asking questions to satisfy his insatiable appetite to know more. 'Did you feel imprisoned on Sicily?'

'No,' Anna replied. 'I was free to go where I liked. The adults who ran the children's house were great. And the neighbours. They knew about who the children were from the time the first ones arrived. They all helped us. I played with the local children. But I was lonely. I longed to have a father and mother like most children have.'

Anna paused and David asked another question, 'How did you leave Sicily?'

She took time for another drink of coffee and to plan the next part of her story. 'It was when I was eighteen. Some people came into my room one night. I could not see them clearly. They kept shining torches in my face. I was told to pack my things. Then we left. The two men who collected me were tall and well-built. They carried guns. We stopped a number of times and stayed with people they knew. I eventually reached the castle which is now my home.'

David was somewhat mystified. 'I thought the Mustermanns were pillars of the establishment,' he said.

'They are. The organisation did not want me to be picked up by any Baader-Meinhof gang members or their friends and indoctrinate me into their ideology. I was therefore kidnapped and taken across Europe, to be housed with an establishment family.'

'So you were imprisoned,' David observed.

'It seemed like it at first. I could not go out. I was very lonely. But I had everything I needed; food, clothes, security. After a time I was allowed out to go to parties and other events people my age attend, under supervision of course! I have had further language teaching since I have been at the castle, in all five languages. The Mustermanns also arranged for me to take courses in office management, business and finance. For a number of years I have been acting as business and financial director to the Mustermann Empire.'

'Why didn't they send you to university?' David asked.

'Too risky! I was never allowed out during the first few years. Then, if I went to an event, it was back to the castle that night. It is only recently that I have been away from the castle for a few days or maybe a week.'

'You told me Franz was your minder. How long has he been doing that?' enquired David.

'Just over a year full-time. Since he left university. Franz was not born when I first went to live with the Mustermanns. I looked after him when he was a baby. As he grew older, we would often talk together. We play tennis, go swimming and play chess together. He is very good at tennis and chess. You have to remember that he is about twenty years younger than me. He has a girl-friend. Since leaving university, he has been groomed to take charge of the family business. I am now considered low risk after being at the castle over twenty years. So now I get to travel with Franz on his business trips.'

'They must be very trusting,' David said, 'I haven't seen him yet.'

'I am sure you will see him before long,' Anna replied, with a smile.

David got up to leave. 'I had better go,' he said. 'Are you paying for the coffees?'

'OK.' She smiled again.

'Oh, could we swap mobile numbers?' he asked. 'We may want to contact each other. We're off home on Saturday.'

Her reply was no surprise to David. 'I think that would be a good idea.'

David left after they had put their mobile numbers into each other's phones.

Emma did not mince her words, 'It's about time you were back. I thought I was going to eat alone.'

'Sorry about that,' David said in a conciliatory tone. 'There was so much to talk about.'

'What sort of things? I'm becoming more suspicious as the days go by.'

'I had better not say at the moment,' said David, still trying to calm the conversation. 'I'll tell you later.'

'How much later?' Emma was looking and sounding angrier. 'Remember what I said at the start about being careful.'

'Yes, I will,' he replied.

Emma was serving the food during their chat. As she became more agitated, so less food reached its destination. David did wonder if some of it might come in his direction. He sat down calmly and started his meal. Emma almost threw herself on to a chair. Her red face said it all. There was now an uneasy silence.

'Don't forget we need to go for a walk earlier this evening. I want to see what they're up to in those fishing boats,' David said. Emma did not answer. At this stage she was not sure if she wanted to go for a walk. She knew he wanted to go and she could allow herself to be persuaded. Then walking along the beach she might be able to find out more about Anna.

A few minutes later, Emma needed no persuading. She had hatched a plot. She was the first to put on her walking shoes. She grabbed a cardigan on her way to the door. David followed her. Perhaps she had calmed down, he thought, and they would be able to engage in some meaningful conversation after all. He was unaware of Emma's devious motive for walking along the beach.

6

SURPRISE! SURPRISE!

I t's cooler this evening,' David said. 'I'm not complaining. It's more bearable than it was at Mont-Saint-Michel,'

Emma added, 'That was a really fascinating place. I wonder why we haven't been there before.'

'Perhaps because of the time it would add to our journey.'

Conversation continued as they walked along the beach. David was pleased that Emma seemed to have left her anger behind; a very welcome change. The taboo topic would be Anna. David certainly wouldn't mention her. He hoped Emma wouldn't either.

In the distance they could see the tractor pulling the fishing boats down to the water's edge. As they drew nearer, they could make out details of what the fishermen were wearing. As they approached the boats, David did not recognise any of the fishermen. Pots and floats had already been loaded into the boats, together with ropes and other tackle. David quickened his pace, with Emma a few steps behind. He was now close enough to cast an eagle eye over the boats.

Suddenly, the peace of the scene was shattered by the sound of sirens. Police cars were speeding down the beach. They stopped in a semi-circular formation at the water's edge. Gendarmes with guns positioned themselves in front of the cars. Other police officers ran to the shore and pulled the fishermen from the boats.

David and Emma were rooted to the spot. It was a frightening experience. Their hearts pounded and blood drained from their faces. What was going to happen to them? They didn't have to wait long to find out. Police officers came from behind and grabbed them by the arms. They led them towards the nearest car, with its rear doors open. They indicated to them to get in. There was no point trying to protest their innocence. There would be time for that later. At this moment, they had to accept they had been arrested.

Emma broke the silence, 'A fine mess you've got us into this time.' David smiled and grasped her hand tightly. Good old Emma, he thought, bringing humour into such a dire situation. She really has become her old self. The car doors were slammed and the vehicle drove off at breakneck speed. Some of the countryside looked familiar to David, what he could see of it. The car continued to make rapid progress along country lanes, with its blue lights flashing and sirens wailing. Other drivers took refuge where they could.

Suddenly Emma remembered something she saw as she and David were being escorted to the police car. 'I'm sure I saw a large black vehicle at the top of the beach, driving away very quickly.'

'When,' asked David.

'When we were arrested and put in this car.'

'I wonder,' David said thoughtfully. 'Will we ever know?'

After what they thought was about half an hour, the police vehicle slowed and turned right and came to a stop. The officers took them by the arms and led them into the gendarmerie. Once inside, they were each interviewed by the duty officer, David first. The few words required were spoken by an interpreter, a petite young lady, who stood next to the officer, clutching a number of folders. David gave his name and address. He surrendered his passport. He turned out his pockets. His mobile and wallet, together with the passport, went into a plastic bag. He was then frisked. His shoes were taken from him and also went into the bag. He was then led down a long corridor by two more officers, one in front and one behind. Shortly before they reached the end of the corridor, they turned left into a small room, containing a desk and a number of chairs. One of the officers gestured David to sit down. Then the two officers took their places standing behind him. When he looked up he noticed a young fresh-faced officer staring at him from the other side of the desk. David assumed he was the interrogating officer. To his left was the interpreter David had seen earlier, still holding the folders. The interrogator spoke briefly to the interpreter and then addressed David.

'Je m'appelle Capitaine Bernard.'

'This is Captain Bernard,' said the interpreter, motioning with her hand.

'Quel est votre nom?'

'What is your name?'

'David Burrows.' The captain opened David's passport and checked the details.

'Quel est votre travail?'

'What is your job?'

'I am a manager for a large financial institution,' said David.

'Une banque?'

'A bank?'

'No, not a bank, but similar.' David felt he had to make sure the facts were correct. He didn't want to be accused of giving false information at a future interrogation.

'Quel est le nom de cet organisme?'

'What is the name of this institution?'

'IFS, International Financial Services.'

The questions from Captain Bernard continued via the petite interpreter. 'Why are you in Normandy?'

'My wife and I are on holiday.'

'Where are you staying?

'In a gîte at Bretteville-sur-Ay.'

'Who owns the gîte?'

'I can't remember.' David's answer caused his interrogator to raise his eyebrows and begin a loud conversation with the interpreter. David understood nothing of what was said, but the tone was obvious.

After awhile the petite interpreter looked at David and said, 'Captain Bernard is surprised you do not know who owns the gîte in Bretteville-sur-Ay. He asks you to think again about who owns that accommodation.'

David knew all the details of the holiday were back at the gîte. He put his hands in his pockets knowing their contents had been taken earlier. 'I'm sorry,' he said, taking his empty hands from his pockets and raising them above the table. 'I cannot think of the name.' The interpreter passed on this information and the questions continued.

'How long have you been staying in Bretteville-sur-Ay?'

'Since Monday.'

'Why were you on the beach this evening?'

'We were going for a walk.'

'Did you know any of the fishermen on the beach?'

'No.'

'Do any of them work for you?'

'No.'

'Have you ever worked with any of the fishermen?'

'No,' said David, thinking this was a strange question.

'Have you been out fishing from this beach?'

'No.'

'You are not a fisherman then?'

'No.'

'Why were you so near the fishing boats?'

'I was interested to see what they were fishing for and what they used as bait.'

'You have been seen in la Haye-du-Puits this week. Is that correct?'

'Yes.'

'Your car has some damage to the front, n'est-ce pas?' David suddenly felt his gut tighten. I'm going to be done for driving a vehicle that's not roadworthy, he thought.

'Yes,' he said.

'How did you damage your car?'

'I didn't. A car drove into me on a roundabout.'

'And what type of car was that?'

'A BMW.'

'A black BMW?'

'Yes.'

'And you have been seen near that black BMW in La Haye-du-Puits this week.' The questions continued apace hardly giving David any chance to answer, 'So are you friendly with the owner of that car?'

'No, not really.'

'What do you mean not really?'

'When I went into Carentan after the crash, I saw a lady near that car. I asked her if she was driving the car when it hit me.'

'And what did she say?'

'No, she was not the driver.'

'Can you describe the lady for me?'

'Medium height, attractive, with dark, shoulder-length hair.'

'Do you know her name?'

'Anna.'

'Did she tell you who was the driver?'

'Yes.'

'And do you know the name?'

'Yes.'

'And what is his name?'

David paused, wondering if he should give the first and second name, or just the first. 'Franz,' he said.

'And what is his second name?'

'Mustermann.'

'And have you met this Monsieur Mustermann?'

'No.'

'Have you ever done business with him?'

'No.'

'Your organisation has never paid money to Monsieur Mustermann?'

Again David paused. If he said, 'No,' and it came out later that money had been transferred from IFS to the German, he could be done for perverting the course of justice. He said, 'Not as far as I am aware.'

'But money could have been paid without you knowing it, n'est-ce pas?'

'It would be unlikely to have happened without my knowledge.'

'Is the lady we arrested with you your wife?'

'Yes, she is.'

'We are interviewing her also. She will be able to confirm all that you have told us, n'est-ce pas?'

'Yes.'

'Why you are in Bretteville-sur-Ay?'

'Yes.'

'And what you have told me about Mademoiselle Anna and Monsieur Mustermann?'

'She hasn't met them, so she will not be able to say much.'

'Have you not told her about Mademoiselle

Anna?'

'Not everything.'

'Is that because it is a secret? Just between Mister David Burrows and Mademoiselle Anna?'

'No!' David spat the word out. 'I've told my wife as much as I think she needs to know.'

'What about the work you do? Is that a secret from your wife?'

'She knows who I work for; that I deal in money exchanges; she doesn't know details of the business deals I do. I have to observe a high level of trust and security.' He said this with considerable anger in his voice. This concluded the captain's questioning. 'Thank you Mister Burrows,' he said.

David had no idea how long the interview had taken. Chinks of light that had infiltrated the room were no longer visible. Captain Bernard got up and left the room, followed by the interpreter. Two other officers continued to stand guard, one inside and one outside the room.

After a long period of inactivity, the sound of approaching footsteps reached David's ears. Captain Bernard entered the room and spoke through the inter-preter. 'We need to check the details you have given us. You will be kept in a cell overnight. If we consider you have not been involved in any criminal activity, then you will be released in the morning. Good night.' One of the guards gestured David to stand up. The two guards escorted him back along the corridor. They put him in a cell, closing the door with a resounding clank. He heard the sound of the key turning in the lock and then the footsteps fading down the corridor.

David laid himself down on the bed. As he looked

around the room, he was close to tears. He then remembered that Emma had gone through, or was going through, the same ordeal as him. She was a strong person, so she would be able to cope with the questioning. But what about having to spend the night in a cell? He knew she would find that very hard. And he wouldn't be there to comfort her. But there was nothing he could do.

He lay awake for a long time. He wondered if his answers would stand up. Had he said too much about Anna and Franz? Would Emma's answers confirm what he had said? Or would they differ markedly? He repeated the questions over and over in his head. He tried to put together some better answers, but it was too late. After what seemed like many hours, he found it more and more difficult to keep his eyes open and he was overcome by sleep.

Emma was put through the same procedure. She always carried her purse with her. It was in her hand when they had left the gîte and her passport was inside. That and her purse, shoes and personal belongings went with her into the salle d'interrogatoire. Emma sat across the desk from a well built, red-faced interrogating officer. Her interpreter was a greying, elderly man, whose trousers fitted him better when he had carried more weight. He was the mouthpiece for the interrogator. Once Emma's name had been confirmed by her passport, the interrogator moved rapidly on to his prepared questions.

'Quel est votre travail ?'

'What is your job?'

'I am manager of a Health Centre.' She wasn't sure if this was accurately interpreted.

' Que faites-vous ici ?'

'Why are you in Normandy?'

'Because we are on holiday.'

'Où logez-vous ?'

'Where are you staying?'

'In a gîte in Bretteville-sur-Ay.'

'Is your husband here on business?'

'No. We're on holiday.'

'Why were you on the beach tonight?'

'We were walking and enjoying the breeze.'

'Is your husband interested in fishing?'

'No.'

'Why was he so interested in the fishing boats on the beach?'

'I don't really know. Last night we walked much later and he missed getting near the fishing boats. Tonight we walked at an earlier time, so he could get a closer look before they went out fishing.' Emma hoped that her full answer would sound convincing.

'What is the job of your husband?'

'He works for a finance company in London.'

'What is the name of the finance company?'

'IFS.'

'What does that stand for?'

'International Financial Services.'

'Does his company lend and borrow money?'

'I think so. I'm not sure about everything the company does.'

'So if someone wanted money, he could ask your

husband for it?'

'I'm not sure. I think it might be businesses that can apply for money. Not individuals.'

'But if your husband needed money, he could get it from his company?'

'I don't think that would be possible.'

'Have you or your husband met any friends since you have been in Bretteville-sur-Ay?'

'No.'

'But your husband has been seen visiting a lady in La Haye-du-Puits, has he not?'

'Yes, once or twice.'

'What is her name?'

'Anna, I think.'

'Is she a friend of yours or your husband's?'

'No. He had never met her before he came here on holiday.'

'So how did they meet?'

'We had a car accident on the way here. The car she was in hit our car. Later he met her by chance in Carentan. She promised to pay for the repair of our car.'

As soon as she said this, Emma realised her mistake. She anticipated the gist of the next question. It came like a bolt of lightning.

'Did any money pass between your husband and Mademoiselle Anna?'

'I don't think so, but I can't be sure. He didn't say he had received money from her.'

'And you don't think your husband has done any business deals while he has been in Normandy?'

'No.' Emma tried to sound confident with her

reply, but she had no idea what had been going on when David had met up with Anna.

'That will be all, Madame Burrows.'

Emma was led from the room by two police officers, like a boxer who had just lost her fight on points. She was put into a cell. The door was banged shut and she heard the key lock the door. Then she threw herself on the bed and sobbed her heart out. Later she paced around the room, slapping the walls. How could David be so stupid, first to get involved with this Anna, then to walk on the beach and get arrested with some local fishermen? And how could I have been so stupid, she thought, and said some of the things I said in the interview? What will happen next? Her emotions were all over the place. Emma returned to the bed and continued to sob. After what seemed like hours she stopped sobbing and she eventually fell asleep. The slightest noise was enough to wake up David and Emma during the night in their separate cells. Sometimes there were noises from inside the gendarmerie, sometimes outside.

As time went by, light began to penetrate their cells. Then suddenly Emma heard the cell being unlocked. The door was opened and a female police officer spoke and used hand signals,

'Levez-vous Mme Burrows, suivez-moi.'

'Get up Madame Burrows. Follow me.'

Emma could hardly get out quickly enough. Then she thought maybe she was going to have a list of charges read to her. She was led into the same room where the first interviews had taken place. This morning a different duty officer was standing behind the desk. There was the petite interpreter by his side. Shortly David was led in and took his place beside

Emma.

The officer addressed them both, 'Nous avons validé les informations que vous nous avez données hier soir.'

'We have examined the information you gave us last night.'

'Il n'y a pas de raison de vous garder ici.'

'There is no reason to detain you any longer.'

'Vous pouvez partir.'

'You are free to go.'

David shuffled about nervously trying to prevent himself from breaking down. Emotions got the better of Emma. She cried out loudly in floods of tears. David quickly put his arm round her shoulder to comfort her.

'On vous accompagnera à votre maison de vacances en voiture. Merci pour votre coopération. Profitez des derniers jours de vos vacances, Monsieur et Madame Burrows.'

'You will be taken by car to your gîte. Thank you for your cooperation. Enjoy the rest of your holiday in France, Monsieur and Madame Burrows.' As the inter-preter spoke these last few words, the bags containing their personal effects were handed over.

7

NEW DAY DAWNING

They were escorted out of the gendarmerie and into a waiting car. Today's journey was slow and dignified, compared to the frantic trip the previous night. No lights, no sirens. It seemed to take forever to get to the gîte, but at last they arrived. David unlocked the door. As soon as they were safely inside, he threw his arms round Emma, who broke down in floods of tears.

'I'm sorry, I'm sorry,' he said. 'It was my fault we got arrested.'

'I thought I may have said too much in the interview,' said Emma. 'Forgive me for that.'

'Let's have a shower and get some breakfast,' David suggested. 'Then we can decide what we want to do today. Sometime we need to look back and see what we can learn from the experience.'

Emma continued to speak through her tears. 'If I'm honest,' she said. 'All I want to do is get packed up and go back home.'

'I realise that, sweetheart,' David said. 'Let's at least make something of our last day here.'

'I know.' She still needed a lot of convincing.

Slowly they extricated themselves from one another. They showered and sat down together for breakfast. Over the meal they exchanged experiences about their night in the cells. 'People won't believe it when we tell them what happened,' Emma said, trying to bring herself to smile.

'I wonder if the tractor left at seven o'clock this morning,' said David. 'We must buy a local paper and see if there's any report about last night.' They agreed that the beach was off-limits, that they should try to enjoy their last day and that they should visit locally and have a meal out somewhere.

'I would like to meet Anna for one last time,' David said. He knew Emma would not like this, so he tried to justify the meeting. 'I want to know what was going on last night. I want to ask her about the black car you thought you saw.'

'I did see,' Emma said. Then she continued, 'Do be careful. We've had enough excitement for one holiday. We don't want anything else to go wrong. Where are we going then?'

'Coutances is a place we haven't visited,' David suggested. 'It has a cathedral. It's not far. And the coast is nearby.' They got in the car and drove off.

'I suggest you keep your speed down?' Emma said. 'We don't want any more accidents, do we?' David agreed, although he thought Emma's advice was a bit over the top.

During coffee in Coutances, they talked about the holiday from the time they left home on Saturday.

'Let's be honest,' David said. 'We weren't in the right frame of mind to enjoy a holiday.'

'I agree,' Emma added. 'We had both been busy at work. Then we rushed around trying to get everything done before we left.'

'Then your question about what makes me love you was a killer,' he said with a frown. 'I must admit I reacted in the wrong way. Before we knew it we were on opposite sides of a great divide.'

Emma tried to be helpful. 'I didn't think I did too badly on the first two days here. I enjoyed it more than I said.'

'That's good to know!' David said with a touch of sarcasm. 'What really put me on edge was the accident. It wasn't bad, but it affected me. Every day I kept thinking about it.'

'What hurt me was you wanting to keep meeting with another woman.' Emma screwed up her face as she said this.

'I'm sorry about that.'

'When we were trying to get our relationship back together, you were never there. You were off meeting her.'

'But it started with the offer to pay for my repairs.'

'Blow the repairs,' Emma said indignantly. 'We could pay that bill ourselves if necessary. You carried on seeing her. You wanted to spend more time with her than with me. Can you imagine how I felt?'

David tried to take the heat out of the conversation, but he realised he was not good in these situations. 'Perhaps I could have handled things differently,' he said. 'All I have done is to have coffee with Anna at a street café. Out in the open. I promise. Certain things she told me have intrigued me. Fascinated me. I haven't felt I can tell you everything now.'

'Is there any relationship between you?' Emma asked.

'No, not sexually. We get on well talking together. She's told me about her background in Germany. I hope I'll be able to tell you the whole story soon. Perhaps when we get home.'

Emma was not convinced. 'And you still want to see her before we go home?'

'You know I want to find out about last night.' Emma had a pained expression on her face. She decided not to continue this conversation.

David tried to pour oil on troubled water, 'As I see it, we have this day together. Let's have a day that I give to you and you give to me. In spite of everything. Let's make the most of this day.' He paid the waiter and he and Emma went off hand in hand towards the cathedral.

'It's huge,' Emma remarked. 'Coutances must have been very important in the past.' The interior was equally impressive. They walked around, largely in silence. Occasionally they spoke in muffled voices, to express their appreciation of all the art and craft that had been brought together in this outstanding Christian edifice.

'Magnificent,' was all David could say as they left. 'Shall we just wander around and look in a few shop windows and see what else the town has to offer?' he asked.

'As long as we don't see her!'

'Unnecessary!' he remarked as he squeezed her hand tighter, to show he thought her words were frivolous and he had not taken them seriously. There seemed to be an improving chemistry between them and neither wanted to spoil that. Eventually they stopped at a restaurant and had lunch.

'You haven't said much about the BMW driver,' Emma said.

'Franz. I've never met him. I know little about him. You know almost as much as I do,' David replied.

'Hmm,' was Emma's response. 'I do keep wondering about what happened last night, to the fishermen, I mean. Where are they now?'

'That reminds me. We said we'd buy a local paper, didn't we? To see if there's a report about last night.'

After lunch, they continued walking down the street and in a few minutes they came across a 'marchand de journaux'. David found the local daily. He held up the newspaper so he could see the headlines and the first paragraph of the report. There was an accompanying photo of a beach scene. That looks like it, he thought. He paid for the newspaper and left the shop.

'Now what are you going to do?' asked Emma. 'Can you read it?'

'No. I'll find someone who can!'

It was not long before David spotted someone whom he thought might help; a smartly-dressed lady in her forties or early fifties. 'Pardonnez-moi madame. Parlez-vous anglais?' he asked.

'Yes,' the lady said.

He held out the newspaper so she could see the article and picture. He smiled and asked her to translate it.

SAISIE DE DROGUE SUR LA PLAGE

Un coup de filet de la police sur la plage de Bretteville-sur-Ay la

nuit dernière. Dix personnes arrêtées. Un porte-parole de la police

confirme les arrestations et annonce que huit d'entre eux sont des

pêcheurs. Les deux autres personnes sont ressortissants britanniques.

20kg de drogue saisis. La police continue ses recherches selon le

porte-parole.

The lady translated it,

'DRUGS HAUL ON BEACH

Police swooped on a group of fishermen on the beach at

Bretteville-sur-Ay last night. Ten people were arrested.

A Police spokesman confirmed the arrests and said that eight

of them were fishermen. Two others were UK citizens.

20 kg of drugs were recovered. Police are continuing

with their enquiries, the spokesman said.'

David stopped the lady when she had reached this point in the story. He gently took the paper from her.

'Merci, merci, madame.'

'Vous êtes les bienvenus,'

'You are welcome,' the lady replied. She watched David with a rather bemused look on her face, as he folded up the newspaper and walked away. He smiled and said, 'Merci,' once more. He was tempted to indicate that he and Emma were the UK citizens mentioned in the story, but he thought better of it.

After looking around other parts of Coutances, David and Emma felt they needed a break from window-shopping. David drove the car to a spot overlooking the beach. The breeze off the sea made the temperature more bearable than it had been earlier.

'I hate to remind you,' said Emma, 'You are going to meet up with Anna sometime this afternoon.'

'Yes,' he replied.

'So how do you meet up with her?' Emma was intrigued to find out how they had met up previously. 'Do you meet up in a certain place at an agreed time?'

'Sometimes we have met up like that,' David said. 'Now I have her mobile number, I can send her a text.'

'So you have her mobile number. In-ter-est-ing!' Emma pronounced the final word in a way that made her sound like a detective who had just uncovered some vital information.

'We both thought it a good idea. For me, at least I have a contact number if I don't receive any money for my car repair.'

'How sensible,' said Emma, introducing a touch of sarcasm into the conversation. 'So tell me, why does Anna need your number?' He ignored Emma's question. He was already busy typing a text to Anna into his phone, 'See you, usual place in 1 hour.' He sent it and put the phone in his pocket.

As he walked towards the café, David couldn't see Anna. There were several older people sitting at tables, and some parents and children enjoying drinks and ice creams. There was only one lady, he guessed, who might be the right age. She had her back towards him and her hair was in a bob. There were few spare seats and David didn't fancy sharing a table with anyone. Anyway, it would be awkward sitting with a lady on her own. He hatched a plan. He would walk slowly past the tables and wait beyond the café for Anna to arrive.

'Aren't you going to sit with me?'

David turned. 'Good heavens!' he exclaimed. 'I didn't recognise you with a different hairstyle.' He stumbled and sat down.

Anna took her passport from her handbag and showed David the photo. 'Anna Mustermann,' he said slowly and quietly. 'That's you!'

'It is nice to have a change,' Anna said. 'I thought I ought to look like my photo.'

'Yes. It's good. It was just a shock at first,' he said. David spoke to the waiter, 'Deux cappuccinos si'l vous plait.' Then he got straight into asking Anna questions. 'Do you know what happened last night?'

'No,' said Anna. 'What happened?'

'Emma and I went for a walk on the beach at Bretteville-sur-Ay. I wanted to take a closer look at the fishermen preparing to go out fishing. Suddenly police cars appeared from nowhere. Gendarmes with guns surrounded the boats and the people that were on the beach.'

Anna looked surprised. 'No, I did not know about this,' she said.

'Emma and I were arrested and taken to the gendarmerie. We were questioned and then kept in separate cells overnight.'

'Poor things,' she said sympathetically. 'So how did you get out?'

'The gendarmes could find nothing to charge us with. So they let us go, at eight o'clock this morning.'

'Some unusual things have happened to you on holiday,' Anna said, with a twinkle in her eye.

'And you knew nothing about this?' David asked. 'And you were not involved?'

'No.'

'As we were being arrested, Emma thought she saw a large black car drive away from the top of the beach. 'Were you in that car?'

'No.'

'What about Franz, was he involved?'

'He could have been.'

'What do you mean, he could have been?' David was getting annoyed.

'I do not know if he was there. It is possible. But I have no evidence to prove it one way or another.'

'The police were looking for drugs. Could Franz have been involved in any way?'

'I think it is unlikely.'

David had now run out of questions about Franz's involvement last night. He opened up the newspaper and spread it on the table. 'There!' he said. 'In the local daily paper.'

Anna looked at the report with interest. 'So, I am sitting with someone arrested by the gendarmes last night! You are mentioned here. It is rather good!'

David was silent. He did not share Anna's excitement about the story. He must not get annoyed again. This could spoil the relationship that had developed between them. 'Hopefully it's all over,' he said. 'The police had no reason to detain us any longer. We can leave the whole episode behind when we travel from Normandy tomorrow.'

'When are you leaving?' she asked.

'Early in the morning. It's a long way.'

'And will I see you again?' Anna asked looking somewhat disappointed.

'Maybe. I'm planning to return soon, to look at the beaches with a friend. But you will be in Germany then.'

'I might be. It depends what Franz has for me to do.'

'I really can't understand what is going on here,' said David. He was getting frustrated and it was beginning to show. 'First you were taken in by the Mustermanns, to stop you being involved in terrorism like your parents. You were closely guarded and shep-herded. You were only allowed out when someone kept an eye on you. More recently that has been Franz. All this week there has been no sign of him.'

'I did say I am no longer considered a risk,' said Anna.

'But you have become company secretary and treasurer. You have kept the business going. You know lots of inside information. They would not want to lose you.'

'I could be replaced,' she said thoughtfully. 'They and I know that one day they will have to replace me.'

'Ah! But not yet,' David said swiftly.

'I will know when the time is right,' Anna said

with a smile. She sounded as if she had everything planned.

'Where will you go? What will you do?

'I think that is enough small talk,' she said, not wanting to discuss this further. 'It just leaves me to say, 'bon voyage'. I hope to see you again.'

David stretched out his hand so it rested on Anna's arm. She moved her other hand to press his hand more firmly to her arm. They looked into each others eyes. A gentle smile rippled across each of their faces.

'It's been good to meet you,' David said.

'And you,' Anna replied, as she stood up. She picked up her bag and walked away. David watched her go. He paid the waiter. Now he had better turn his thoughts to Emma.

That evening there was no time for protracted discussion about their marriage. Emma was busy with packing. David tried to tidy up the gîte, by putting things where he thought they belonged.

'One last walk?' he asked.

'Not on the beach!' she replied.

'But it's hardly scenic, walking amongst the gîtes.'

'OK, so it's no walk,' Emma said triumphantly.

David checked the car. Then he loaded up as much as possible. They climbed into bed early.

'I need a good night's sleep after last night,' David muttered.

'At least the bed is more comfortable,' Emma said. 'Don't forget about the tractor at seven o'clock.'

'I'd forgotten about that.'

8

DOWN TO EARTH

As it turned out, they were up before six o'clock the next morning and left the gîte well before seven. David did take one last look out of the bedroom window. There was no sign of activity. The tractor stood idle. He was not going to wait till seven o'clock to see if anything happened.

'We will never know if anyone drives down to the beach this morning,' he said.

'Or whether the fishermen are still in police detention,' Emma added.

As they joined the road leading to La Haye-du-Puits, they both became silent. They had their own reasons to reminisce. The occasions David had met with Anna in the town flashed through his mind. He remembered the feeling of euphoria afterwards as he negotiated the narrow lanes on his way back to Bretteville-sur-Ay. What did the future hold, he wondered. Emma only remembered the manic trip in the police car, her interrogation, and then the terrible night in the cell. She was glad to be leaving it all behind.

It was cooler on the way back than on the way to Normandy. There was less traffic. They passed Carentan and Bayeux, and crawled around Caen. The bridge over the River Seine was less congested than on their previous visit. David pulled off the A29 into a service area to get diesel, coffee and have a rest. Then it was on the road again, with a lunch stop at Abbeville.

Sometime on the second leg of the journey David felt his mobile vibrate. He checked it in Abbeville and found he had a text from his daughter, Sue, 'How R U? We haven't spoken for ages. Sue x.'

He got up from the table, saying, 'I'm just going outside to give Sue a ring.'

'Hi darling. We're OK,' David said.

'Have you had a good time?'

'Yes. I'll ring you when we get home.'

'We were concerned,' said Sue. 'We couldn't get through on either of your mobiles. Speak when you get back. Bye.' David rang off.

Once back at the table, David outlined his conversation with Sue. 'I said we'd ring when we're home.' During lunch, David admitted to feeling tired. 'I think the past few days have taken their toll. At least we can have a good break here.'

'Are we nearly in Calais?' asked Emma.

'We've done about two thirds of the journey. What time are we booked in?'

'Four o'clock French time.'

'Should be fine,' he said.

The only hitch was getting to the Eurotunnel check-in. Sat Nav Jane said, 'Go straight on,' when it was obvious to David that he should turn left. The cost of obedience for him was to find out he was leaving the terminal.

'Silly woman!' he muttered. 'Turn her off. We can make our own way to the check-in.'

A second message came in when they were in the queue for the Shuttle. He checked it. 'Hi David. Hope you've had a good break. Where R U? If you're back this evening, can U give me a ring? I need to come and see you. Brian.'

'I wonder what my boss wants.'

'Must be important for him to contact you now,' Emma said.

David sent a message to say that after 7pm would be fine.

All the administrative formalities were quickly completed. The train journey was smooth and gave time for a quick bite and a drink. Traffic on the motorways was heavy, but there were no hold-ups. It was not long before they pulled into their drive.

'Home, sweet home,' exclaimed David.

'I'm pleased to be back.' Emma added.

'At last we can have an English cup of tea,' he said, putting the kettle on. 'I'll just give Sue a ring. Do you want a word when I've finished?'

'Yes, OK.'

'Hello, Sue. I'm sorry about the break in communication while we were away. All beyond our control. We weren't aware we couldn't contact you. So how are you, Tom and the children?'

'Good.'

'Kids enjoying school holidays?'

'Yes. How was France?'

'I was coming on to that. We got hit by a car on a roundabout. It put a dent in my front wing. I can sort that out now I'm home. The other thing that happened was that we spent a night in the cells in a gendarmerie. We were walking on the beach. The police grabbed us. They put us in a car and off we went. No lasting damage,' David said. 'Hi Tom. We're not really criminals! No, we're not committed to anything tomorrow. OK, that would be great.'

David handed the phone to Emma, saying, 'They've invited us for lunch tomorrow. I'm off to have a shower.'

After Emma had finished speaking to her daughter and son-in-law, she put the receiver down and the phone rang almost immediately. 'Oh! Hello Brian. Yes we're back. Seven o'clock is OK for you? I'll tell David. See you soon.'

When Brian arrived David was already hovering by the front door to let him in. 'Good to see you,' David said. 'Bit of a surprise on the day we arrive back from holiday! What are you going to have to drink? Wine, beer, tea, coffee?'

'I'll have a coffee if I may,' Brian replied.

Emma had been waiting in the hall. She gave Brian a smile and went off to the kitchen to make the drinks.

Brian sat himself down on the sofa and said, 'I'm not going to find this easy. I'll not beat about the bush. While you were away we had a snap inspection. Men in grey suits crawling all over the building. As a result, they found a hole in the finances. I'm sorry to say it was in your department. On Thursday I had to tell them

96

not to come in with immediate effect, unless requested to do so.'

'I don't know what to say,'

'About what?' Emma asked, as she entered the lounge carrying a tray of drinks.

'All my department at work has been suspended,' David said. Then to Brian, 'Any idea how much?'

'I'm not at liberty to say. I will let you know on which day the inspectors would like you in for questioning.'

David and Emma were shaken and it showed on their faces. It was as if the events on holiday were not bad enough. This was the final straw. Brian made a feeble attempt to reassure them that all would be well. As he got up to leave he said, 'I'm sorry to be the bringer of bad tidings. I'm sure it will all be sorted quickly.' With that he left.

As he walked to his car, Brian felt pleased with himself. He had carried out his mission well. It was never going to be easy to tell one of his underlings bad news, but he had done it clinically and without getting emotionally involved. It was a good performance.

David sat there with a puzzled look on his face. 'He didn't even drink his coffee,' he said. 'I didn't have my beer either, but I will now. He didn't ask about our holiday.'

A long period of silence followed, during which they both thought deeply about the implications of what Brian had told them. They continued to sip their drinks. David was the first to break the silence.

'As far as I'm aware everything was balanced

when I left last Friday. I can't understand what could have happened.'

'But there's nothing you can say or do until you get summoned to appear next week,' said Emma.

'Summoned is right,' David said angrily. 'I'm on trial. I'm in charge of eleven others and I'm getting the blame. What could have gone wrong?'

Emma tried to reassure him. 'One good thing is that you're still on holiday next week. Nobody will notice any difference because you're not at work.' This was no real comfort. He felt he had been hit hard, both mentally and physically. Coming on the heels of the two experiences on holiday, his confidence had been badly shaken. He downed the last of his beer, got up and went outside.

The soil around the plants was moist, so there was no need to do any watering. He would collect Smudge tomorrow. He couldn't cope with doing that now. The only thing that consumed his mind was the situation at work. It was like a nightmare had come to life. He began to question his ability to cope. By the time David went back indoors, Emma had tidied things away and was making her way upstairs. He followed her and they crawled into bed like battle-scarred soldiers.

As they lay there wondering how long it would take to get off to sleep, Emma ventured a thought out loud. 'Do you think anyone has got it in for you? Is someone trying to put the blame on you?' she said.

'I shouldn't think so,' David answered. 'We have a good team. We're usually reliable and achieve good results. I say that, but after this last week, maybe anything could happen!'

David felt utterly wretched when he woke the

next morning. A vast array of thoughts assaulted his mind. How could it happen? When did it happen? Why did it happen? And inevitably, why me? He had assured Emma last night that there was unlikely to be a conspiracy against him, but now doubts were creeping in. Could there be a link between a car accident in France, being arrested by the gendarmes, and money going missing from IFS. It was ridiculous to entertain such thoughts, but was there any connection? At present he could do nothing to find an answer, but the whole sorry saga consumed every part of his being. He felt like a prisoner on death row, not knowing which was to be the day of reckoning.

Emma disturbed his thoughts. 'Have you had breakfast?' she asked.

'I've had a cup of tea. I couldn't eat anything,' he said. 'I'll ring the cattery and arrange to pick up Smudge. Then we can set off for Essex. What do we tell Sue and Tom? We can tell them about the accident and getting arrested. They're almost funny compared to this latest scandal. What do we say about that?'

'Just say that while you were away there was an investigation at work,' Emma suggested. 'You'll let them know more when it's over.'

'That sounds terrible. It will arouse suspicion. Best not to say anything.'

Sue welcomed her parents with hugs and kisses when they arrived. 'You don't look like two people who spent a night in a police cell. You don't have any signs of stress.' David thought that nothing could be further from the truth. At this point the grandchildren came wanting to be hugged and kissed. They took grandma and grandpa into the garden, where Tom was putting together a slide, to go with the other play equipment.

'Hi! Good to see you back safe and sound,' said Tom. 'We want to hear all the details of what happened to you in France.'

Having had two goes on the newly-assembled slide, Rachel then thought it was grandma and grandpa's turn. 'No sweetheart, we're too big,' said Emma. 'You have another go.' The grandparents were rescued from any further attempts to get them to try the slide by the arrival of coffee. David and Emma told the story of their car accident. Then they gave details of their ill-fated walk on the beach, which ended with their arrest, interrogation and having to spend the night in the cells.

Emma took a newspaper from her handbag and spread it on the table. 'There was a report in the local paper,' she said. 'It says that ten people were arrested on the beach at Bretteville-sur-Ay, on suspicion of being involved with drug smuggling. Eight fishermen and two people from the UK; that was us. Fortunately no names, no pictures.'

David continued the story. 'They released us the next morning; once they had realised we had no connection with the fishermen or drugs.'

As Sue was collecting the coffee mugs, Emma said, 'Your dad has something else to tell you.' David's heart began to pound; he wondered what Emma was going to say. He thought they had agreed to say nothing about the investigation at IFS. 'About a lady called Anna,' she continued.

'Oh la la,' said Tom. 'Tell us more.'

David felt like a fish on a hook. Somehow he had to free himself. He spluttered to begin and then got into his usual confident stride. 'Actually she was German. She was in the BMW that hit us on a roundabout. I saw the car later that day. Then I met Anna while I was taking photos of the car. We talked about the accident. She told me about herself…'

'Over several days,' Emma added.

'I don't want to say any more. Her background is a very tangled web.' A palpable silence followed David's closing words. Tom went off and joined Sue in the kitchen. David thought the best thing he could do was to go and encourage Rachel and James on the slide. This left Emma alone on the patio, to ponder the impact of her words.

Conversation over lunch was mainly about the other half of David and Emma's family, son Steve and his wife, Jo, and their daughter, Fiona. After the meal Emma and David offered to wash up.

'You don't need to,' said Tom. 'We can put every-thing in the dishwasher.' After a cup of tea, which they drank in silence, Emma and David bade their farewells. David had a quick handshake with Tom and kisses for Rachel and James. When he came to Sue, they both had tears in their eyes as they hugged and kissed each other.

Once they were on the road, David had a go at Emma.

'Why did you say that? For a minute I thought you were going to say something about me being suspended from IFS. When I realised you were referring to Anna, I felt you were setting me up as someone who'd embarked on a seedy holiday romance. You didn't have to say anything. So why did you?'

'I thought Sue and Tom ought to hear the story from us first, before they hear it from someone else.'

'Who else are they likely to hear it from?' David asked sharply. Emma didn't reply. The rest of the journey passed in uneasy silence.

When they arrived home, David said, 'I'm going out for a quick drink.' He hoped that time with his mates and a few drinks would help him put his suspension to the back of his mind. It would also help him forget about his deteriorating relationship with Emma. The episode over coffee was the first time for a long time she had made him appear foolish in front of other people.

David spent a convivial evening in the pub. He recounted stories of the car accident, and his meeting with Anna, briefly. There were lots of laughs over the arrest of Emma and David and the night they spent in the cells. There was much leg-pulling and jovial banter. But at the end of the night, David had to face the fact that he had a knife in his back. He knew who had put it there and it was starting to open a large wound.

The next morning David and Emma conversed briefly over coffee. Yesterday's heavy atmosphere persisted. The weather was more overcast, but still hot. David decided he would tidy the garden and cut the lawns. Emma said she would find out about the fete from Mrs Smith and visit Pat and Maureen. She hoped to be back in time for lunch.

When David came into the house at the end of the morning, he discovered he had an answer machine message from Brian. He rang him immediately. 'Thanks for returning my call,' said Brian. 'We have now set up a complete programme of interviews during this week. Could you make yourself available on Wednesday morning from nine o'clock?'

'Yes OK,' David replied.

'For about an hour,' added Brian.

'Yes,' he said again.

'I will see you then.'

Over lunch David and Emma engaged in small talk. They avoided any mention of their crumbling relationship. David gave details of his interview with the inspectors at IFS on Wednesday. He did this in such a way that he gave the essential information without allowing the opportunity for further discussion.

'I'm planning to go to Oxford tomorrow,' he said. 'Do you want to come?'

'I've got a lot of things I need to do here,' Emma replied. 'I'll have to shop for food sometime. And I've promised Sally I'll go round for coffee in the morning.' So that's a 'no', David thought.

David always appreciated having a passenger with him on a long journey. It took away the monotony of the road. It was someone with whom to share time and conversation. Today there was nobody with him. Driving on the M25 on a Tuesday morning was never likely to be pleasurable, but it could have been worse. Traffic came to a halt as he neared the M40. Apart from that, he had a good journey to Oxford. He stopped at a Park and Ride off the A40. The bus trip into the city centre was a convenient way of travelling. David considered he was doing his bit towards saving the planet. It also saved his money and his nerves.

Once in the centre of Oxford, David found a suitable café on the High Street. He would have preferred to sit outside on a day like today, but this café looked friendly and inviting. As he sat down, a man on the next table smiled and nodded to him. To David he looked to be in his 40's, with hair going grey at the temples. He was casually dressed, so David thought perhaps he was on holiday. David ordered a latte and a pastry. He was aware that the other man was watching him closely. When the waiter brought his coffee, David took the opportunity to have a longer look at the man on the next table. He could not be sure, but he thought he recognised him.

'Burrows, Shirebrook 75-82,' the other man said. This confirmed to David that they had met before.

'You have a good memory,' David said. 'I'm David Burrows. What's your name?'

'George Stebbings. I recall you played rugger. The most active game I played was chess.' They both smiled. 'Why don't you bring your coffee and join me?' David took up the invitation.

'I hope this won't cause confusion when it comes to paying the bill,' David said with a grin.

'The worst that can happen is that I have to pay for both of us,' George replied. 'So what brings you to Oxford? Are you on holiday?'

'Not exactly. I've come to love and treasure this city of the dreaming spires over many years. My wife and I have some wonderful memories of times we've spent here.'

'Is your wife with you today?'

'No! She's at home.'

'So where is home?'

'Penshurst in Kent.'

'Another beautiful part of the country,' George added.

'Do you live in Oxford?'

'In Wheatley. Not far away.'

'Do you work in Oxford?'

'Yes. At the university. I came as a student and I have never left!'

'What is your subject?' David asked.

'Economics.' What do you do?'

'I work in London for International Financial Services as a departmental manager.'

'So you're one of the people who caused the financial mess we're in,' George said with a wry smile.

'I hope I'm trying to sort it out, giving stability to banks and the money markets.' David hoped he had put the record straight. He didn't want to say anything more, with enquiries going on at work and his interview the next day. He changed the subject.

'Are you married?'

'Sadly I'm not any more,' George said. 'My wife died of cancer five years ago. We had no family, so I'm on my own now.'

'How do you find that?'

'I'm getting used to it. Colleagues and friends have been very good. I get invited out a lot. But I'm often the only single there. Then when I go home, there's no-one there with whom I can share my experiences. I don't have anyone to help me with problems that come up in life.'

David almost wished he hadn't asked George about his wife. On the other hand it had given him a chance to talk. And it had made David think about his own situation; how fortunate he was to have a close supportive family, even though his relationship with Emma was presently at rock bottom.

George spoke to end an uneasy silence. 'What about a stroll round part of the city? I could show you a few places you may not have visited before, some of the colleges for instance. I'm not an official guide, but I do have thirty years experience of living and working here.'

David did discover some places in Oxford that he had never seen before. George was able to reveal some of the history and modern developments of the city. He took David into the college where he spent most of his time. They stopped for lunch at a restaurant that George said had a good reputation. The conversation over lunch was mainly about memories of their school days.

'Shirebrook was a strange place, stuck in the middle of the countryside,' David said.

'The locals considered us boys a load of toffs,' added George. 'We were shut away for weeks on end and only allowed out for holidays.'

'There were occasions when we could go into town,' David said, 'but these became opportunities for bad behaviour, often involving girls or beer.'

George recollected that some boys from the year above had been expelled. There were various rumours about what actually happened. The two of them agreed that the punishment meted out was ostensibly to keep peace with the locals, rather than to be a fair response to the crime.

'I have no contact with anyone from the school now,' David said. 'Do you?'

'No. Perhaps it's not surprising. You spend all that time with a number of boys for seven years. Yet when you leave, the friendships mean nothing.'

'It's like that with people I knew at university,'

David went on. 'Even mates I played rugby with every week. I do see one or two of them from time to time, but we're of an age now when our playing days are over. There's no longer any reason to meet up. What about you, George?'

'I do see a number of colleagues from years ago. Oxford and the university are so vibrant. Events go on all the time. Purely by chance I am likely to meet past acquaintances.'

'It has been good to meet up with you today,' David said. 'Whether by chance or pre-ordained.' George agreed. They swapped addresses and added each other's number to their mobiles. They parted with a handshake and expressed the wish they would see each other again.

By the time David arrived home, Emma had already had tea. She was doing some embroidery in the lounge. He made himself a sandwich and put it on a plate with an apple from the fridge.

'Would you like a cup of tea?' he asked as he switched on the kettle.

'No thanks, I only recently had a coffee.'

David took his food and drink into the lounge and settled himself into an easy chair.

'When I was in Oxford today I met someone who was in the same year as me at school.'

'Interesting,' Emma replied.

'He lectures in Economics at the university.' Emma was far more interested in her embroidery and stopped listening to what David was saying. He changed the subject to try and regain her attention. 'After I've finished this, I'll look through a few papers ready for tomorrow. Then I'll have an early night. I'll be away early in the morning.'

David was uncertain whether his wife was listening to him or not. He was getting no response, so after eating his apple, he went out into the kitchen.

9

WHATEVER NEXT?

David was up early. He just couldn't sleep. He would leave on a later train than usual and that would still give him plenty of time. He had to stay relaxed and do things slowly. He must not feel pressured. He arrived at Tonbridge station in good time. There were no familiar faces.

When the train arrived there were few spare seats. David sat down beside an older lady wearing a flowery dress and sporting a large smile.

After a few minutes she opened conversation. 'Off to work?' she asked.

'No I'm not actually,' David said. 'I'm on holiday, but I have to go in for a meeting.' That was as much as he wanted to say.

'It must be a very important meeting if you've been called back from your holiday,' she observed.

'Yes it is,' he replied, hoping that would be an end to that topic of conversation. 'So what brings you out so early to go to London?

She smiled and said, 'I'm having tests on my cancer. And some more treatment.' David was lost for words. She went on, 'The doctors and nurses are marvellous. They give me all the time I need. They explain all about what they're doing for me. Sometimes they keep me in for a couple of days, just to keep an eye on progress.'

David had to butt in, 'But shouldn't you be in an ambulance or a hospital car?'

'I do sometimes,' she said, 'but I try to be as independent as possible. And I can save money by using my rail card.' Again she smiled.

David thought he must ask, although it was rather insensitive of him. 'I know it's rude, but how old are you?'

'Eighty-eight! What about you, young man?'

'Fifty.'

'A mere youngster,' she said and laughed to herself. 'So what's your name, young man?' she asked with a twinkle in her eye.

'David.'

'Such a nice, straightforward name,' she observed.

'What's your name?'

'Barbara,' she said, with a flutter of her eyelashes. 'I've always been happy with it, so I think I'll keep it for now!' She gave something between a smile and a grin. 'So where do you live, David?'

'In Penshurst.'

'Such a lovely part of the country. I used to live in Sevenoaks a long time ago. Now I live in Baldslow, near Hastings. Such a strange name for a place, isn't it?

'Yes it is rather.' David was uncertain if he had

heard the name before.

'And do you have a wife in Penshurst?'

'Yes, I do.'

'I'm sure she is very beautiful, and loving and kind.'

'Yes,' he replied with a slight nod of the head. But not at present, he thought. 'Do you have a husband?'

'No, sadly not,' said Barbara. 'He died during the Second World War. He was a paratrooper at the Battle of Arnhem. He was shot almost before his feet touched the ground. He was nineteen.' The smile was gone from Barbara's face for the first time since they met.

David was hurriedly thinking of something appropriate to say, but 'I'm sorry,' was all he could manage.

'That's alright. People were very good and supportive. It was a difficult time.'

'Did you have a job?' he asked.

'Yes, I was a teacher, helping those who found school difficult. I was Akela for the local cubs for some years. My little boys, I called them. They made up for the family I never had.' Now the smile was fully restored.

David thought over the things Barbara had told him. He was feeling knotted inside about the coming interview, which should cause him no problem. Then there was this little old lady, who had had a difficult life and was having treatment for goodness knows what type of cancer and she managed to smile all the time. This put everything into perspective.

David and Barbara continued to talk and she continued to smile. At times Barbara would break into laughter and even David managed a smile. It was not long before the train started to pull into Charing Cross. The time seemed to go so quickly, David thought. If only there was a Barbara in the next seat on every train journey!

'I hope everything goes well at the hospital,' David said.

'I'm sure it will,' she said, giving him one of her biggest smiles. 'I do hope your meeting doesn't go on too long and you can enjoy the rest of your holiday.'

'Thank you for sharing the journey with me,' he said, as he helped Barbara down to the platform. They shook hands and made their way towards the barrier. He thought he should have given her a hug, but perhaps that would not have been appropriate. As they moved on they were engulfed by other commuters. They became more separated from each other and then she was gone. As David came out of the station and walked to IFS he said to himself, 'What an incredible woman,' over and over again.

David entered the International Financial Services building and spoke to Sarah in reception.

'Hello, David,' she said. 'It's a pity you had to break your holiday for this.'

'What has to be done has to be done,' he said. 'I hope this can all be cleared up as quickly as possible. I'll tell you about Normandy sometime. We're at home doing odd jobs this week.' Turning back to look at Sarah he said, 'Where do I have to go?'

'Go and make yourself comfortable in the lounge. The interviews are being held in the small meeting room on level 4.'

David had just put down his briefcase and taken a

seat, when an attractive lady entered. She was dressed in a grey suit and her hair was in a bun. She looked to David like the personification of efficiency.

'Mr Burrows?' she said. 'Please come this way.' As she opened the door to the interview room, David saw three men sitting behind a large table. In front of them, some distance away, was a solitary chair. David felt so nervous. He had never felt as nervous as this, not even on his wedding day. The man in the middle, whom David assumed was the chairman of the panel, gestured for him to sit down.

'Thank you for coming, Mr Burrows,' he said. 'You realise that we are here to investigate the disappearance of a sum of money, which we discovered had gone missing when an inspection was carried out last week. You, being the manager of the department where the loss occurred, are held responsible.'

David spoke up, 'You will be aware that I was on holiday when this inspection took place and when the loss of money was discovered.'

'We were aware of that. Because of your absence, we were not able to speak to you last week.'

One of the younger investigators took over the questioning. 'How long have you worked at IFS, Mr Burrows?'

'Over twenty-five years.'

'And you have always been happy here?'

'Yes, extremely happy.'

The third man then asked, 'And for how many of those twenty-five years have you been manager of the department?'

'For the last twelve.'

He continued with his questions, 'How many work in this department?'

'Twelve altogether, including me.'

The chairman then continued questioning David, 'Do you think you run a happy team?'

'Yes, I think so,' David said with a smile.

'How well do you know the members of your team?'

'Most of them have been here during the time I have been manager,' David replied. 'I would say I know them very well.'

'Would that be outside the office, as well as working here for IFS?'

'Yes.'

'Knowing them very well, as you say you do, would you say that any of them are in financial difficulty?'

'Not as far as I am aware,' said David.

'Have any of the team joined IFS more recently than the others? Say in the last five years?'

'Kevin Watts joined us in 2010, so four years ago. Ian Philips joined last autumn.'

The chairman was keen to find out more about these more recent employees. 'Do they both integrate and socialise with others in the team?' he asked.

David replied, 'Kevin Watts, yes. Ian Philips less so, I would say. He rarely comes along when we all go out for a drink. He starts his lunch break after most of us. Then he comes back when we are back at work. It must be difficult for him. He's much younger than the rest of us. He seems to find it hard to fit in.' David had tried to tell things as they were. He didn't want to sound too critical of Ian.

'Now,' the chairman said, 'when you finished work to go on holiday, nearly two weeks ago, you were sure that everything was in order, correct?'

'Yes. I had discussions with a number of the members of my team on that Friday. I checked every-thing was in balance before I left.' David was confident about this.

'So any discrepancy must have occurred while you were away?'

'Logic tells me that is the case.'

Investigator two then shifted the focus of the ques-tions, from the office to David himself. David found this unnerving as the investigator looked straight at him and asked, 'Tell me, Mr Burrows, do you have any difficulties with your personal finances?'

'None whatsoever,' David said with confidence. He felt angry the question had to be asked.

The chairman quickly continued this line of enquiry. 'Can you explain why £5,000 was paid into your bank account in the last few days from a German bank?' David was surprised by this revelation. He paused to collect his thoughts before answering. The chairman used the silence to give what he considered could be damning information, 'It may help you to recall the transaction if I tell you the payee's name was Mustermann.'

David regained his composure and spoke with assurance. He explained about the accident and the promise made by Anna that the Mustermann family would pay the invoice as soon as the repair was completed. 'All I can think is that the money was paid in advance as a good-will gesture, to show that the promise would be kept.'

The final few questions were about technical issues concerning the way checks are carried out and balances arrived at. The chairman asked David if there was any way that someone could override these checks.

'I think it is very unlikely.'

The chairman concluded the interview, 'Thank you, Mr Burrows, that will be all for now.'

David left the interview room and went into the lounge, where he made himself a cup of coffee. He felt confident with his performance. He was perhaps a bit unsure of his assessment of Ian Philips. The real hammer blow had been the payment of £5,000 into his account by the Mustermanns. What was that all about? he asked himself. Am I the one suspected of corruption? Was Franz involved in some way with drug smuggling on the beach at Bretteville-sur-Ay? Was Franz trying to frame him? There were so many questions to which David needed some answers, desperately.

While enjoying his coffee, David came up with a plan for the rest of the day. He would browse around some of the shops he walked past every working day, but had never entered in twenty-five years. Then he would have a substantial lunch, whatever the cost. On the train he would find another 'Barbara' to speak with on the way home. Unfortunately for David trains leaving Charing Cross in the middle of Wednesday afternoon were not as crowded as commuter trains from Tonbridge during the rush hour. There was no shortage of seats. Those travelling on their own were either glued to their headphones, working on a laptop, or holding endless conversations on their mobiles. The only possibility was a plump lady of about sixty, cradling a dog in her arms. David refused this challenge, as he didn't want to get mauled by a Chihuahua! The last event he planned was to go to the pub and have a drink with his mates. He drove straight to the pub from Tonbridge station. He had a great time and drank far too much. He had to wait for a lift to be arranged for him and he arrived home in the early hours of Thursday.

Emma was busy in the garden by the time David emerged in the middle of the morning. When she heard him moving around in the kitchen, she came indoors.

'I'll join you for coffee,' she said. Then she remembered the real reason for pausing from her gardening. She resumed with a sharper edge to her tongue, 'What time did you get in this morning? I know it was this morning! I was working late and I didn't get to bed till after midnight. There was no sign of you then.'

'I'm not sure what time it was. I know it was the wee small hours. John brought me home.'

'So did you drink in celebration or to drown your sorrows?' Emma asked.

'Neither. Perhaps to celebrate it was all over.'

'When will you hear what's going to happen to you and your department?'

'Nothing was said. I'll just have to wait and see.'

Emma continued with her questions. 'What have you planned to do today?

'I must give 'The Bodyworks' in Tonbridge a ring to see when they can repair my car. Slipped my mind with all that's been going on.' Then remembering his car was still at the pub David continued, 'Can you give me a lift to The Chafford Arms to pick up my car?'

'Can't one of your drinking mates do that? After all, they helped to get you into the state you were in!'

David thought an explanation was long overdue. 'In no way was I drunk last night. I knew I had downed enough to put me over the limit. I asked and John volunteered to bring me home.'

Emma felt she had lost the argument but only if David was telling the truth. She would continue to hold the high moral ground and bargain her way to a winning position. 'I'll see if I can fit you into today's programme,' she said. 'I want to finish that piece of garden before lunch. I need some shopping. I said I would have a cup of tea with Maureen mid-afternoon. If I say I can be available towards the end of the afternoon, how would that suit you?'

David knew Emma was being awkward, but he took up her offer. It was likely to be the best she would make!

Emma said nothing on the journeys. By the way she was behaving, David did not think she was trying to mend their marriage. On the contrary, she seemed to be going out of her way to make things worse. When they arrived at The Chafford Arms for David to collect his car, Emma marched straight in and addressed the landlord.

'Why did you continue to serve my husband last night when he was already drunk?' she asked. 'Then he couldn't drive home.'

The landlord spoke calmly and slowly, 'Mr Burrows asked if someone would give him a lift home, as he was probably over the drink-drive limit. He thought this through himself. He was not drunk. He is an honest man.' With that the landlord picked up some empties and retreated into the kitchen behind the bar. This left Emma alone, to rue what she had said and to realise her embarrassment had been self-inflicted.

The receptionist at 'The Bodyworks' had asked David to take his car in before five o'clock. He made it with minutes to spare. His car would be ready Monday or Tuesday.

It was fortunate for David that his friend rang that evening and asked him to play mixed pairs golf the next morning. Peter knew Emma didn't play golf, so he had asked a friend, Rachel, to partner David against him and his wife. At least a round of golf would take his mind off other things, he thought.

David then rang his friend, Paul, to see if they could meet up sometime to talk about their proposed trip to Normandy. David excitedly described the beaches, museums and cemeteries he had recently visited. Paul was guarded in his response. He had to be frank with David. 'I know this is something we've talked about for sometime. But with things being difficult at work, I won't be able to get time off this autumn. Later, perhaps,' he said.

David knew Paul had always been lukewarm about a trip to Normandy. He was therefore not too surprised about Paul's decision. After coming off the phone, he sat and thought. He would have to make his own plans to go back to Normandy. Maybe, if he was still suspended, this could be sooner rather than later.

Soon the phone rang again. It was Clive, a long-time friend from Crowborough. It had been some considerable time since they last met up. As the telephone conversation developed, David remembered a 'do' that he and some friends had attended, but Clive had sent his apologies because he wasn't well. David felt a twinge of conscience that he hadn't got in touch with Clive to see how he was. Now Clive was phoning him to invite him to come over to his cottage.

'Can you come and see me Saturday afternoon or evening?' Clive said. 'Bring Emma if she'll come.'

'Hang on a minute,' David said, 'I'm without my car at the moment. I'll have to borrow Emma's. I'll go and speak with her.'

Emma was watching a film on the television in the lounge. As David entered, she motioned for him to be quiet.

'I've been invited to go and see Clive in Crowborough Saturday afternoon or evening. Can I borrow your car?' Emma paid more attention to the film than to her husband. She continued with her finger to her lips and said, 'Shh' repeatedly.

David mimed that he was on the phone. 'I've got Clive on the phone. Can I use your car on Saturday?'

Emma shifted her attention from the television to David. 'I'll need it all morning,' she said. 'You can have it after lunch.'

'So I can go and see Clive Saturday afternoon?' he asked.

'Yes, but I might need it Saturday evening.'

David was exasperated and it showed. He confirmed that he would see Clive Saturday afternoon. Then he replaced the handset. He went back into the lounge. 'You annoy me intensely,' he said. 'I want to borrow your car on Saturday afternoon to meet an old friend. All you can do is to watch television and wave your arms about and make far more noise than me.' Emma said nothing. 'What sort of impression did that give to Clive, do you think? Why did it take you so long to decide? I think you're going out of your way to be difficult.'

Emma continued to maintain her silence. The film had now finished, so she switched off the television. Then she picked up the used cups, saucers and plates from the lounge and took them into the kitchen and took herself off to bed.

10

LIVING WITH THE ENEMY

The mixed pairs golf went well. Rachel was a good player. David thought she was a few years older than him. He imagined her forty years ago wearing blouse, skirt and knickers, playing hockey and netball for the school, and perhaps tennis and squash in local clubs. She had a good strong figure. At times she chided herself for playing a poor shot. She and David made a good pair. However Rachel spent most of her game with a stern look on her face. David found she was not easily drawn into conversation. On the fourth hole he asked her advice about where he should put his second shot. She replied, 'It's for you to decide. It's your shot.' When Rachel made a par 3 on the eighth with an excellent putt, David congratulated her. She took no notice of his compliments and set off for the ninth tee with the same stern look on her face. After a few more rebuffs, David gave up trying to engage her in conversation. Although David and Rachel played a good, steady game, they were no match for Peter and Angela Meadows.

Peter took the occasional opportunity to speak with David as they moved around the course.

'I understand things are not too bright at work,' he said, as they walked one of the fairways.

'Where did you hear that,' David asked.

'Not sure. Someone remarked that your problems at work were having an adverse effect on your marriage.'

David was angry, but he tried not to show it. He certainly had no intention of speaking in public about his matrimonial difficulties, nor was he willing to comment on the situation at work. 'There is an investigation going on at IFS at the moment and when that is completed we will be able to distinguish truth from speculation,' he said with authority, bringing closure to the conversation.

On walking to another hole, Peter posed further questions to David about his marriage.

'Is Emma alright?' he asked. 'We haven't seen her for a long time.'

'She's OK. She's under lots of pressure at work.'

'Angela and I were only saying the other day that we haven't seen you and Emma out together for ages.'

David delivered his prepared reply, 'It's not been easy for either of us recently, with the pressure we've both been under at work. I'm hoping things will change for the better once these difficulties are behind us.' As he said this, David felt far less confident about the situation than his words were intended to convey. He hoped his answer would set Peter's mind at rest, if only for the present.

At the close of the match, Peter and Angela were

declared worthy winners. Back at the clubhouse, David and Rachel bought the drinks. They would go down well with the salads they had ordered before the start of play. Afterwards Rachel was the first to leave, without saying a word. As David and his opponents walked to the car, Peter apologised to David.

'You can't have a good lady golfer and a good conversationalist, I'm afraid!'

Peter pulled his car into David's drive. David removed his bag from the boot, then bade farewell to his friends. As he walked up the path, he felt good. It had been a pleasant morning on the golf course and the exercise had done him good. The thing that annoyed him was that he and Rachel had lost. Being very competitive, that hurt!

David dropped his bag in the hall. Emma heard him come in and emerged from the kitchen-diner. She was ready for him.

'I suppose you've had a good time, while I've been working my fingers to the bone, looking after this place,' she said, making a gesture with her hands. David could see she was angry. He wondered what had brought this on. He was in no mood to get drawn into an argument, so he said nothing.

Emma continued her verbal bombardment. 'I had a phone call from Baileys about painting the outside of the house. I don't know what you've arranged, do I? You'll have to sort that out.'

David moved into the lounge, so he could relax in an easy chair. Emma followed him to continue her onslaught and sat on an upright chair. She picked up the local weekly and threw it across the coffee table towards him.

'Where did that come from?' she demanded.

David glanced at the paper. He could hardly believe his eyes. There was a photo of him and Anna. The headline read Kent couple arrested in France. The brief report went on to say, Mr and Mrs Burrows were arrested while on holiday in Normandy, accused of smuggling drugs. They were taken to the local police station to be interviewed.

David took several deep breaths before he spoke.

'I have no idea about this. I can't think.'

'You'd better start thinking quickly,' Emma snapped. 'Who's that woman?' she asked, pointing her finger at the paper.

'That's Anna.' David felt that soon he would have to tell Emma more about Anna.

'When was that taken?' Emma asked with anger in her voice and fire in her eyes.

'It wasn't! I have never had my photo taken with Anna.'

'So how do you explain this?' She produced an envelope and withdrew a photograph. She threw it in David's direction. It landed at his feet. He picked it up and saw it was an enlargement of the one in the paper. He studied it carefully. In the photo Anna had long hair, so it was taken early in the week when he had met her. He tried to work out when the photo of him was taken. He concluded that it was while he and Emma were in Normandy. Who took it? Did Anna have a camera? One thing was for sure, at no time had he and Anna been standing side-by-side posing for a photo.

After several minutes David gave a careful response to Emma's questions.

'Looks like a composite photo of two people,' he said. 'Made to look as if they were together when it was taken. How did it get here?'

'By post. Envelope franked in Germany.'

David offered an explanation. 'I think it's been done as a joke. I might have an idea who sent it.' He placed the photo on the coffee table, only for Emma to snatch it up again. She tore it in two, separating David from Anna.

'It's no joke to me. People will see that in the paper and ask who that is and why I'm not shown! It's going to ruin my credibility. What will people at work think?'

David continued to speak in a calm, measured tone.

'What's done is done. We can't undo it. The best thing we can do when people ask us about the photo and the article is to say we did get arrested and then released without charge. The photo is fictitious.'

Emma's anger had risen once more. 'My future is on the line,' she shouted. 'I don't know how I will face people again.' With that she rushed out of the lounge, tearing the photo of Anna into little pieces as she went.

David sat there, thinking over what had been said. Was the photo sent to Emma as a nasty practical joke, or was there an evil motive behind it? As he pondered these thoughts, he leaned forward and picked up the brown envelope. The only clue to its origin was the German business postmark. He wondered about that too.

There was now a terrible atmosphere between Emma and David. He kept out of Emma's way by going out into the garden to cut back some of the shrubs. She spent most of her time in the lounge feeling angry and betrayed. He wished he had his car, then he could go for a drink at the pub. Emma had said he could borrow it on Saturday afternoon. He wasn't going to push his luck and ask to borrow it today as well.

David came in at the end of the afternoon, cleaned himself up prior to making tea. During the evening he continued reading the novel he started on holiday. Some of his favourite music played gently in the background.

Emma was up early the next day and had gone out before David came down for breakfast. He cleared the table and then set about catching up on letters, phone messages and emails he had ignored for too long. He knew Emma would continue to nag him until he had dealt with every single one. He didn't want her to have any more grounds for complaint. By the end of the morning lots of paperwork still remained to be done. There was no sign of Emma, so David prepared lunch for himself. He had almost finished by the time Emma arrived home. She put in a brief appearance to make herself a drink. Although she wasn't crying and her cheeks were no longer red, she had a dishevelled look about her. Recent events had taken their toll.

David was looking forward to seeing Clive in Crowborough. Their friendship went back a long way. David considered him a real friend, who would stand by him through thick and thin. He would be there when others had withdrawn their support. He picked up Emma's keys from the hall and left the house, whistling a merry tune to himself. There was no point dwelling on things that had happened. He must look forward with optimism. As he adjusted Emma's seat, he remembered her saying that she might need her car tonight. He thought that was unlikely seeing the state she was in. He considered he had the car for the rest of the day.

Clive lived just outside Crowborough, in a cottage with an ample garden. David enjoyed meeting up with him, especially when it was at Clive's place. He was something of a rustic character. His garden was meticulously cultivated, flowers at the front and vegetables and fruit at the back. He also had a modest greenhouse and a large shed. The latter was adjacent to his cottage and in it Clive would create a large number of objects out of wood.

David thought Clive was several years older than him. He had an unkempt appearance. His hair looked as if it could do with a good comb. His beard had not been trimmed for a long time. Clive did not fit into the clean-cut mould that Emma approved of.

Clive had worked as a design engineer with the Royal Navy for a number of years. He had a brilliant mind. He could always be relied upon to come up with a solution to any problem. He designed and made gadgets to make life easier and he also made a number of 'fun' things that were appreciated by children and adults alike. Not only were the finished articles important, but Clive derived an enormous amount of satisfaction as he produced them.

Clive had been doing a bit of weeding in the flower garden before David arrived. The sound of tyres on the gravel made him look up and then straighten himself. He walked forward with outstretched arms to greet his old friend.

'Excuse the dirty hands. It's good to see you again,' he said.

'I'm pleased to see you,' David said. 'You don't

look a day older than last time.'

'Give me a minute to wash my hands, and then I'll make some tea. He emerged from the kitchen drying his hands on a towel, which was long overdue for a wash. He sat down opposite David at the table. 'Now, how are you, David, my friend?'

'I'm alright.'

'Sounds to me you're not top-notch,' Clive observed. 'So why is that?'

David gave a brief résumé of the situation at IFS, adding that he hoped things would be better soon.

'And what about your good wife, Emma?'

'She's not well at the moment. She's under a huge amount of pressure at work. They've given her more to do than she can cope with. She's now at breaking point.' The whistling kettle cut short the conversation.

Soon Clive shuffled back from the kitchen with two cups of tea. 'Sugar?' he enquired.

David shook his head.

'I've been sugar-free for years,' he said triumphantly.

Clive returned to the discussion about Emma.

'The human body can only do so much. I know. I've been there. If you try to make it do more, it rebels and shuts down. So what are Emma's long-term prospects of getting back to normal?'

'I'm not sure. Being manager of a Health Centre makes it difficult for her to say she can't do the job. Who would she go to?'

'But there must be something that can be done to help her out of the pit of despair,' Clive said. 'You have an important role to play in supporting her through this, my friend. She needs the support of a good husband.' David understood this, but he could think of one hundred and one reasons that prevented him from supporting Emma.

As the discussion went on, David was trawling his mind about Clive's marital status. He could never remember Clive having a wife. He wondered if Clive had been married and his wife had died. Certainly, whenever a group of friends had met for a party, Clive had always been on his own.

'Right!' said Clive clapping his hands. 'I'd like to show you some of the things that have exercised my brain this year.' Saying this, he got up and walked out of the back door, and then along the path to the greenhouse. 'I've come up with this irrigation system for my tomatoes,' he explained. 'There's a network of plastic tubing under the compost. The pump is driven by these solar panels. It takes water from the tank outside and passes it around the tomato plants.'

David thought he had discovered a flaw in the system.

'What happens if there's no sun?'

'I simply run the motor from the mains!' Clive exclaimed with an air of triumph.

'You're incredible,' David said. 'Quite a boffin!'

'Or a buffoon!' joked Clive. He closed the greenhouse and led David back towards the cottage.

'Before I show you my thingamabobs, I must go and put the oven on. You will stay for something to eat, won't you?'

David nodded and said.

'I look forward to it.' He never intended being

home early enough for Emma to use her car.

Clive quickly returned and ushered David into his shed. There were bits of wood in various shapes, sizes and colours, waiting to be fashioned by Clive's creative skill. There were also many works in progress. Scattered amongst these on the work benches were assorted cups, other trophies and certificates, together with some photographs. David was drawn to one framed photo, depicting Clive sitting at a table, which was covered with a variety of wooden objects. The caption read, GET YOURSELF A THINGAMABOB.

Clive picked up a selection and showed them to David. There were door stops, trinket boxes, and tongs; polished apples, pears and oranges; bowls of different shapes and sizes; a selection of knives, forks and spoons; mushrooms and toadstools gaily painted in primary colours. David could only stand in awe of his friend, who had created all of these. His curiosity got the better of him.

'Why thingamabobs?' he asked

'It's what you call something when you can't remember its name!'

As they returned to the cottage, the beautiful aroma of cooked meat teased their nostrils.

'I'll just go and put the veg. on,' said Clive. 'Will you have a glass of wine with your meal?'

'I had better not. I can't risk being over the limit.'

'Hope you won't mind me having a glass! Water is OK for you?' David nodded.

'So what are you serving up?'

'Beef cobbler, with vegetables sourced from the cottage garden. Dessert is summer fruit tart with cream or custard.'

'That really does sound good,' David said. 'I'm sure it will taste good too!'

Over the meal, the two friends continued to talk about Clive's skill in making things out of wood. Clive went on to explain.

'During my work, I mainly designed and made things out of metal. But I've always had this fascination for wood.'

'So do the thingamabobs give you an income?'

'Not really,' Clive replied. 'I do it because I enjoy it. What money I make goes to good causes locally.' David admired his friend's unselfish attitude. It was refreshing to hear him say he was working to help others, and not seeking financial gain or glory for himself.

While Clive cleared away the plates and dishes from the first course, it gave David the chance to run his eye quickly around the room. It had basic furnishings and there was no television. This suggested Clive lived far more frugally than he and Emma did. Dessert was as good as the main course. Clive persuaded David to join him for coffee before he set off for home.

'I hope Emma's health improves,' Clive said. 'Tell her from me that she must slow down and stop running herself into the ground. Help is available if only she knows where to look.'

'Thank you for giving me such an inspiring time here,' David replied. 'I look forward to seeing you again soon.' As he walked towards Emma's car, he wondered when their next meeting might be.

As David walked into the hall, he could see no sign of Emma. He did a perfunctory check downstairs. As he climbed the stairs, he noticed the master bedroom door was wide open. A quick glance inside confirmed she was not in there. The spare room door was closed. Should he assume she was in there? Maybe! Perhaps she had been invited out, with the offer of a lift home thrown in. Should he try the spare room, just in case? David knew he wouldn't be popular if he woke Emma up. He went downstairs, hoping that Emma was fast asleep in the spare room.

David turned on the television and did some channel-hopping. None of the programmes grabbed his attention. After a while he turned the television off. He was just about to go upstairs when the phone rang. Ah, he thought as he crossed the lounge and picked up the handset. 'Hello,' David said. After a long pause, the caller answered.

'It's Brian. Sorry to call you so late.'

'I did wonder who it might be at this hour.'

Brian spoke softly, trying to sound reassuring. 'Come in to work as usual on Monday morning.'

'So is it all over?' David asked.

'Not exactly. It's now a police case. I will meet all departmental managers first thing on Monday and tell you all what has happened. I will give you some guidelines, so each manager can run a tighter ship.'

'Thanks for letting me know,' said David. 'I'm pleased I'm no longer implicated.'

'I will say something about that on Monday,' replied Brian. 'Good night.'

'The old sod,' David said to himself as he put down the phone. 'He really has got it in for me!'

11

INFIGHTING

David was awakened by the alarm. He got up straight away. The first thing he had to do was to find out what had happened to Emma. As he came down the stairs he could hear the sound of the radio coming from the kitchen. Emma was sitting at the table.

'How are you, darling?' he asked.

'Much better,' she replied. 'Sleep is a great healer. You were right. The past is gone. The future is what I need to concentrate on.'

Emma looked better than David expected. Certainly it was good to see her sitting there, after all the scenarios that went through his mind last night. He was the first to break the uneasy silence.

'I thought we might go for a drive somewhere, to enjoy time together before we get back to work.'

'That's a good idea,' Emma said. 'But are you going back to work?' She gave him a quizzical look as she asked the question.

'Yes. Normal time tomorrow.'

'What happened then?'

'I don't know. We're all being told in the morning.'

While they walked on Box Hill, David felt a text arrive on his mobile. He thought it came from one of his mates, maybe suggesting they should meet up for a drink. He waited until he returned home before he checked the message.

'The time is now. Meeting Point at St Pancras 7.30pm. A.' What did this mean, he asked himself.

Over a cup of tea, David asked Emma if he could borrow her car for the evening.

'Final fling and all that,' he said.

'That's OK,' Emma told him, 'but please don't be late.'

'I won't. I need to make a good impression, remember!'

David drove to Tonbridge and then caught a train to Charing Cross. So far, so good, he thought, as he approached the London terminus. The underground to King's Cross took longer than he had hoped. He made a quick dash to St Pancras and was in position by 7.15pm. You've done well, he congratulated himself. Anna was pleased to see him. They found space at one of the cafés and ordered drinks. More than anything, David was eager to hear what was going on.

'So why are you here?' he asked Anna.

'I'm here with the blessing of the family. They know they cannot keep me for ever.'

'Where are you staying?'

'I have somewhere just around the corner. It

comes recommended. I have set myself a week to obtain a job.'

'I see,' said David thoughtfully. He was not sure if having Anna around in London for a week was a good or a bad thing. His thoughts then shifted to yesterday's showdown with Emma.

'What do you know about my wife receiving a black and white photo of us together?'

'Nothing at all,' Anna said. 'Where was it taken?'

'I don't think it was. It looks like two photos have been made into one.'

'I know nothing about it,' Anna said emphatically.

'OK. I promise I won't ask again.' David quickly changed the subject. 'Where are you hoping to get a job?'

'There is a post to head up the Policy Team at IFS,' she said. David looked at her in amazement. Seeing the expression on his face, she added, 'But I will not be applying for that. I am not that stupid! I do have some other contacts to follow up.'

As the conversation was coming to an end, they arranged to meet up after work the next day. David suggested having a meal at a restaurant in Charing Cross that he and his colleagues had used. Anna was happy with this and took her leave.

Emma was still preparing for work when David arrived home. 'Can you drop me off at the station in the morning?' he asked. 'I may have to stay in London later than usual.'

'Yes, OK,' Emma replied. 'How will you get home?'

'Probably have to get a taxi.' David thought he would be pushing his luck to ask Emma to pick him up.

David went to bed in an agitated state. He was restless and found it difficult to get off to sleep. He tried to empty his mind of everything to do with IFS. Time after time thoughts of going back to work flooded back in.

The next day, as the train neared the end of its journey, David began to feel nervous. His mouth was dry and his stomach in knots. It felt like he was starting a new school. The headmaster had directed that he report to his study, along with a few other boys. There they would be reminded of the rules and how they should behave. Stories were told about former miscreants as a warning. David pictured himself standing there in short trousers. The headmaster, dressed in a black suit and gown, was parading himself in front of the boys, cane in hand. From time to time he would point at a particular boy with his cane, to remind him of the rule being explained. He spat out his words with relish. It was a frightening experience, David remembered. It took him a long time to recover from it. Surely Brian wouldn't be like that. He had known David for years and they had always got on well. But Brian and the upper echelon had been rocked by this scandal. They would need to introduce new procedures, to ensure that nothing like it ever happened again.

David approached reception, where Sarah greeted him.

'Good morning, Mr Burrows,' she said cheerfully. 'Brian is waiting for you in the meeting room.' David discerned that change was already under way. Brian met him with a handshake in the doorway. He indicated for David to sit on one of the chairs, which had been arranged in a semi-circle. Some had got there early. Others continued to arrive and take their seats. When the last person came in, Brian closed the door and sat himself behind an impressive table facing the managers.

'Good morning,' Brian began. 'It is good to see you all. Thank you for coming.' The smile faded from his face and his words became more formal. 'You all know what has happened at International Financial Services recently. This is why you are here today. I can reveal that Mr Ian Philips, a trainee in Mr Burrows' department, has been arrested and the matter is now in the hands of the police.'

Brian picked up a piece of paper and moved it across the table. He continued, 'What Mr Philips did was to try to make money for himself by dishonest practices. Mr Philips invented a fictitious account. He transferred £5,000 into it from one of the accounts he had been working on.' It was likely that David was the only manager who understood the significance of this amount of money.

Brian continued his revelations. 'After a few days Mr Philips planned to transfer the money into his personal bank account. Then he would close the new account he had created and hope his crime would go undetected. Fortunately for us, his actions were discovered during a routine inspection and the enquiries which followed. This episode has demonstrated the need for greater oversight and safeguards to be in place in each of your departments and in Mr Burrows' department in particular.' These words angered David.

'This happened when I was on holiday,' he shouted.

Brian addressed David directly.

'Thank you Mr Burrows. I will complete my statement about this unfortunate matter.' Then looking at all the managers he said, 'I will give details of the changes which will be introduced from now on. Then I will invite observations and take questions.' As he spoke, his eyes went around the semi-circle of managers. 'As I was saying, greater oversight and safeguards need to be put in place. If someone is away, particularly a manager, someone else needs to be responsible for carrying out checks. A chain of responsibility will be introduced, so each of you knows where you stand. This whole sorry business has the potential to ruin International Financial Services. This time it was £5,000. What would have happened if it had been £50,000, £500,000, or £5 million? Our reputation is at stake. People will want to know we have taken swift action and introduced procedures, so this can never happen again. I think this is all I want to say at present. I will, of course, be speaking with each of you individually over the next few days. Now, would anyone like to say anything or ask a question?'

David had been slapped down once. He was not prepared to be humiliated again. The ensuing silence indicated that none of the others wanted to share his fate. When it was obvious that nobody wanted to say anything, Brian thanked them for coming and closed the meeting. There was much muttering as the managers left and went along the corridor.

David had to somehow pick himself up and regain his confident managerial poise before he entered his department. He put on a brave face as he went round to each of his colleagues. He told them about Ian Philips. They thought he might have been involved, as he was the only one not at work. Over lunch David regaled his work mates with stories about his holiday in Normandy. He made much of the arrest and imprisonment by the gendarmes. He spoke of the beaches and cemeteries. He said nothing about encountering Anna.

Throughout the afternoon David's mind went back over the meeting with Brian. The way it went indicated that he was the scapegoat. Ian Philips would eventually be charged by the police, but it looked as if someone wanted David's head to roll. He had been loyal to IFS for more than twenty-five years. The reward for this loyalty was to get a slap in the face. Should he be looking for another job? Should he have been looking for years? He couldn't wait for the afternoon to end and to meet up with Anna again. Before he left the office he gave the garage a call to find out when his car would be ready. He was told to collect it on Tuesday before 5pm.

Anna looked her bubbly, beautiful self, when they met at the restaurant. She was keen to tell David about the places she had visited, and the businesses she had contacted concerning employment. From the things she said, David thought she had not been to London before. He remembered the burning question he had intended asking the previous night.

'I have something to ask you,' he said. Anna looked a little anxious. 'I recently discovered that £5,000 had been paid into my account from a German bank. Do you know anything about this?'

'No. Should I?'

'Your links with the Mustermann family and German banks suggest you might.'

'On this occasion your ideas have led you to the wrong conclusion,' she said.

When David told Anna that his planned trip to Normandy was unlikely to take place, she showed little interest. Before leaving each other, they arranged to meet briefly at lunchtime the next day. As they parted, Anna kissed him gently on the cheek.

The taxi from Tonbridge dropped David off at the end of the drive. He did a few sprightly steps to the front door. He poked his head into the lounge and found Emma sitting on the sofa, looking tired and drawn.

'What sort of day have you had?' he enquired.

'Not good,' she replied.

'Why? What happened?' David wanted to find out more, but he realised he had to be so gentle.

'Going back to work was bad enough. Then there were the questions about the holiday. Why did we get arrested? Questions about Anna. "xxxxxx" Anna! I wish I had never heard of her. I wish I'd never gone to France. I wish we hadn't been hit by that car. I wish I could die!' These last words shook David. Emma started making wailing sounds and then she cried uncontrollably. He wasn't sure if this was real or fake.

'Shall I make you a cup of tea?' he asked. Emma continued to cry. 'What did you have for your tea,' he said.

Through her tears she managed to blurt out, 'I didn't have any tea. I couldn't eat anything. I feel so wretched.'

'Have a hot drink. That may help you.' Emma shook her head. All she could do was to feel sorry for herself.

'What's going to happen tomorrow?' David's question caused Emma to shed more tears, accompanied by more wailing noises. He thought she was putting on a good performance.

David went to the kitchen and made himself a coffee. He still hoped to encourage her to have a drink. By the time he went back to the lounge, Emma's major bouts of crying were over. Again she refused to have a drink. She continued to mop her eyes with a tissue, while her other hand supported her head.

'I think it best if you go to bed,' he said, 'otherwise you won't be fit for anything in the morning. C'mon, I'm going up when I've finished my drink. I need an early night after a hectic day.' Emma shuffled towards the door. She made her way up the stairs with ponderous footsteps. David watched her. He was concerned for her state of mind and what she might do to herself.

12

GATHERING STORM

The next morning was dull and dreary. Emma failed to respond to her husband's prodding. He thought there was no way she would be going to work. He would borrow her car to get to the station. Then he would give the health centre a call, to let them know Emma was too ill to come in.

David's meeting with Anna at lunchtime was a brief affair. He did have one question he had been pondering.

'When you're away on a trip like this, do you stay in contact with the Mustermann's?'

'Sometimes I do and sometimes I do not,' Anna replied. 'It depends if they need regular feedback on the business I am conducting.'

'And what about this time, on your trip to London?'

'They have advised me on contacts to follow up.' Anna paused. Then she took a drink of wine. 'Herr Mustermann would like to meet you sometime,' she said.

Interesting, thought David.

'I could be free a few days in September,' he said. 'That's when I had intended going back to Normandy.'

'I'll see what I can arrange,' she said.

As they got up to leave, David's mind re-focused on his problems with Emma and the difficulties at IFS. He said, 'I am under great pressure at the moment. Things at IFS demand my complete attention. I won't be able to see you any more this week.' Anna looked crest fallen. She said nothing. David pulled her towards him and kissed her passionately. She gave him a broad smile and whispered, 'I think I understand.'

Before going back to his office, David phoned Emma at home. He needed her cooperation to get her car back to the cottage. There was no reply. He tried her mobile and left a message.

Once back at work David found a memo from Brian on his desk. It put in writing the guidelines he had spoken about at the managers' meeting on Monday. David lost no time in having a word about the guidelines with each member of his team. They were a loyal bunch and he wanted to keep them on board a happy ship. He also had to deal with a difficult client situation that was still unresolved at the end of the afternoon.

On his way home, David had a call from Emma. She had made arrangements for her car to be brought home. David went to The Bodyworks to collect his Mondeo. They had done a good job. He paid by card and set off for home. When he arrived, Emma's car was already on the drive. He entered the cottage and found Emma in the kitchen making a cup of tea.

'Would you like one?' she asked.

As David looked her up and down, he could

hardly believe his eyes. She looked smart and attractive and full of life.

'What's happened to you?' he asked. 'This morning I couldn't rouse you. Look at you now! Looking lovely and full of energy! It's nothing short of a miracle!'

'After you'd left,' Emma said, 'I thought if I didn't shake myself, I could stay in bed all day. I got up and dressed. I rang Pat to ask for a lift to work. Things went well. I had a good meeting about drafting new Conditions of Employment for the Trust. After work Pat ran me to the station to collect my car.' Emma carried on talking while she busied herself around the kitchen. 'I'm not having a meal tonight. I'm going out with some of the girls. I've got cottage pie out of the freezer for you.'

David found it difficult to believe what he was seeing and hearing. Later Emma took herself upstairs to change and do her make-up. When she came down, there was even more of a transformation. She picked up her jacket and bag from the bottom of the stairs.

'I'll try not to be late,' she called out. Then she left, slamming the front door as she went.

Emma had looked forward to this evening out with friends, from the time someone suggested it earlier in the day. Pat, Beryl, Sandra, Jackie, Wendy, Jean and Emma. They had been friends for a long time, since they met at play group, when their children were babies and toddlers. They had supported each other through all the problems life had thrown at them. When a child was poorly and had to go into hospital, some of the other ladies would provide meals and look after the rest of the family. Two of the friends had suffered from cancer.

They had been encouraged through their operations and treatment by the others. Three ladies had experienced wobbly patches in their marriages. It was the loving support of their friends that had enabled them to weather these marital storms. Although things had been very rocky at times, the three ladies took pride in the fact that they had managed to keep their marriages intact.

These seven friends were like a big family, always there for each other. Emma had often taken the lead in organising help and support for one of the others. Now it was her turn to be on the receiving end of 'family support', as she faced problems in her marriage and the Chinese whispers about what happened in Normandy. Yesterday it was people who didn't know Emma very well who were asking difficult questions and drawing the wrong conclusions. Tonight Emma was amongst friends. She told them about the run-in with the gendarmes and being held in a cell overnight. She spoke about the car accident and how it led to David meeting Anna. Most of the questions which followed concerned David and Anna.

Jackie asked, 'So did David meet her a number of times?'

'Three or four,' said Emma.

'How did that make you feel?' asked Beryl.

'Brassed off,' came Emma's reply.

Wendy ventured to ask the question at the back of each of their minds.

'As far as you know, was there a sexual side to the relationship between David and Anna?'

'I should think not. It's very unlikely. They met up in cafés and car parks in broad daylight.' Emma's answer was greeted with hoots of laughter.

As the discussion continued some of the friends suggested that Emma should have planned a full programme each day, so David had no time to meet with Anna.

'We always had to come back early from a trip so David could see her,' Emma said. Other friends thought David was a 'lovely man', who could be trusted. He had been a great friend to each of them and they appreciated this. Emma didn't want this to turn into a David Burrows appreciation society. She thought she ought to add a touch of caution.

'David has a wandering eye as far as the ladies are concerned. He has a way with women. I'm not sure I would trust my granny with him!'

This was met with a chorus of dismay.

'He's always been good to me,' said Beryl. Sandra spoke about David paying her compliments about her appearance.

'Richard and I will always be grateful to David for the help he gave Richard when he lost his job,' said Jean. As similar expressions of gratitude were voiced, Emma realised she was in a minority. It had been good to be out with the girls, but by the end of the night Emma felt jaded. It's alright for them, she thought, but I've got to be married to him.

Sandra gave Emma a lift home. As she stopped her car at the end of the drive, Sandra said, 'I hope we'll be able to meet up again soon.' With a quick wave, she drove off. There was no sign of David, so Emma assumed he had gone to bed. That could mean he was well ahead in the snoring stakes. At least there was the spare room if things got too noisy.

Over the days that followed, there were major challenges for David and Emma. These served to push their marital problems further down the list of priorities. David's intractable problem with a client continued. After a lengthy phone call, he felt he was at last making progress. Then the door opened and in walked Brian,

'Just come to see if you got the note about the guidelines,' Brian said. David was seething, but tried to stay calm. He felt like a naughty school boy, who had done something wrong and had been caught and punished. On this occasion he knew he hadn't done anything wrong, but he realised he was now under surveillance and his every move was being monitored.

'Yes, I've had a word with my department. They're all keen to conform. They don't want to be singled out for special measures in future,' David said sarcastically.

'Oh, good, good,' Brian replied.

'However, I do have to say I get the feeling that I'm being made a scapegoat. That my job is on the line.'

'No, no,' said Brian. 'It's just part of the top brass plan to plug any loopholes. So there are no more scandals.' David was unconvinced. Brian used to be a friend, in spite of him being his superior. Now David was being treated as inferior, like an office junior. More and more he thought that his days with IFS were numbered.

'OK,' David said, 'I'll do my best.' With that Brian left. This was another sign of the worsening relationship between the two men. A few weeks ago Brian would have stayed to ask after Emma. Not today. David thought he should look around to see what was available sooner rather than later. One thing was certain; David would say nothing to Emma.

Emma was in the midst of her own crisis. A year ago a young boy had died, because of the failure to diagnose the seriousness of his heart condition. Emma felt the boy and his family had been badly let down. Communication problems had occurred at the Health Centre when a new IT system had been introduced. This had been a key factor in the failures which took place and ultimately led to the boy's death. The story had rumbled on in the local papers and on television for months. The CEO had issued a statement at the time. Now he was off work with stress and Emma had been asked to take on some of his workload. At the inquest, the coroner had blamed the death of the child on the NHS Trust, for improper diagnosis and a failure in communication.

Emma became the spokesperson for the NHS Trust. She had to appear before journalists and cameramen to apologise. Her explanation sounded feeble and unprepared. She found it difficult to hold herself together while on air and then afterwards. She couldn't get back to her office quickly enough. There Pat found her in a terrible state, sobbing her heart out.

'Poor you,' Pat said, 'you did very well.'

'What could I say?' sobbed Emma. 'The only thing was "sorry". I think I saw the parents in the crowd. It was awful.'

'One thing, you're not driving home. I'll take you.' Pat continued to offer Emma sympathy, support and coffee. When she deemed Emma fit enough, she drove her home.

David had been home sometime when Emma arrived. He had made himself a cup of coffee, and then looked around the kitchen for clues about the evening meal. Finding none, he thought Emma must have it all planned.

Emma slammed the front door and made straight for the lounge.

"xxxxxx" NHS,' she said. 'What a terrible day I've had!'

'What's gone wrong?'

'The result of the inquest was published today. About the little boy who died.'

'Sorry. I didn't realise that was today.'

'The coroner criticised the Trust. I had to read out an apology. It didn't sound convincing.'

'I can't really know what this feels like for you,' said David. 'I've been put through it at work. Nothing like this. You poor thing.'

David thought Emma looked numbed by the whole experience. She was back where she had been a few days ago. 'What had you got in mind for a meal?' he asked.

'I hadn't got as far as thinking about that.'

'Shall I go out and get something? Or do you want me to rustle something up?'

'I don't mind. Up to you,' said Emma, kicking off her shoes and putting her feet up on the sofa. 'I don't want much.'

David put some fish and chips in the oven. He and Emma decided to eat in the kitchen-diner. 'Wine?' he asked.

'I'll have a white.' David also poured one for himself.

'We're no further forward on making our marriage work,' he said as they ate.

'Trouble is, there's been no time, with all that's been going on,' Emma observed.

'And neither of us have felt like talking,' he said, with a wry smile. 'Your experience today would not have been affected one way or the other if our marriage had been strong. You were the one who had to go through with it. There was nothing I could do to help. It would have been nice to know that it was taking place though.'

'But the other issue,' Emma said, 'would have worked out differently, if our marriage had been strong.'

'You mean the events in Normandy?'

'Yes. Forget about being arrested and spending the night in a cell. The thing that really hurt was your affair with another woman.' Emma felt justified in her description. She couldn't believe David and Anna spent their time drinking coffee when they met up.

'It wasn't an affair,' David said emphatically, although he knew this was a lie.

'Call it what you like, you were seeing another woman!'

'That started as I attempted to get the repairs to my car paid for.'

'You've explained that before and you sound no more convincing. Where's the affair now?'

David looked serious.

'So how would a stronger marriage have helped in that situation?'

'If you were full on for me, you wouldn't have been looking at any female you fancy.'

'At times I have been full on for you. You've taken no notice of my advances and spurned my affections.'

Now it was Emma's turn to scowl. After a long silence she said, 'We've spoken about this before. I feel less passionate than I once did. That's how it is.'

'Is there anything I can do to help?'

'I don't know. I don't think so. Even when I go out with the girls, I feel so alone, in spite of being in a crowd. I just don't feel as happy as I once did.'

'Would it be worth having a word with one of the doctors? They know you well, perhaps too well.'

'Good try, but no. I don't want to do that. Bare my soul before whoever I see.'

'It might be the best way forward,' said David. 'You're not the only one who has felt like this. There are bound to be others.' He tried to come up with other helpful suggestions without success.

Emma got up from the table and began to stack crockery into the dishwasher. 'When I've finished this, I'm going to bed to read.'

David seized the opportunity. 'When one of us goes to bed early, the other one carries on with what they are doing and goes upstairs much later. Why don't we try to go to bed at the same time? That could help improve things.'

13

DREAMLAND

David hadn't heard from Anna all week. He had hardly used his mobile. When he got up, he took the mobile from its case and switched it on. There was one new message. It read, 'Watch this space! A.' It had been sent the previous day. He sent a reply, 'OK!'

That night David experienced his dream again, but this time it had become a nightmare. The basic scenario was the same as before. Once again it involved German soldiers standing guard across a cobbled street. No one was allowed to go past them. Some people were inquisitive to know what was going on. They were curious about what the soldiers were guarding. In the past, if someone ventured too close, a soldier would raise his rifle and the person would withdraw. Tonight if a person took a step too far, he or she would be shot by one or more of the soldiers. The sound of rifle fire brought more people out on the streets, anxious to know what was happening. These were ordinary men, women and children. The increase in numbers caused greater chaos. More people dared to go nearer to the soldiers and lost their lives as a consequence.

As David was able to take a closer look at the victims, he realised they were people he knew, personal friends and family members. When he could take no more of this, he bellowed, 'No,' at the top of his voice. It woke him up; he was shaking and bathed in sweat. For a time he sobbed uncontrollably. The noise woke up Emma, but she didn't let on she was awake. After some minutes David had calmed down. He tried to think when he first experienced this dream. It began several years ago, perhaps when he first started making plans to visit the D-Day beaches. He then started researching what his father and uncle had done in World War Two. He had always assumed the dream was set in a French village. He had never recognised the village on any of his holidays in France. The pattern of the dream was similar on each occasion, except tonight. What had brought about the change? Why were his friends and family shot dead? Gradually David settled down for sleep once more. He pulled the covers over him for greater protection. He assumed Emma had slept through the whole episode.

On Friday night David received a text from Anna, 'Meet me in London tomorrow. You say where & time. I have lots to tell you. A x' He replied, 'I can't. E will get suspicious. See you for meal in Charing + after work Mon. D x'

When they met, Anna told David her news with great excitement.

'I have been offered a temporary part-time job,' she said. 'That is not good enough. I have told them so. I will keep looking for a full-time permanent post. In the meantime, I have some work to complete with the Mustermanns. I will be in Germany shortly.'

David was thankful to get a word in.

'You are definite about working in London?'

'Yes, to gain experience, if only for a short time, but I need to finish my contract in Germany.' Anna then launched into her next exciting piece of news. 'You remember I said Klaus Mustermann, Franz's father, would like to meet you. When I got back home, I told him that you worked in finance in London. He asked me lots of questions. He asked me to arrange that you go over to see him. He has proposals to put to you. When I leave, he will need a David Burrows as my replacement.'

David wasn't sure if he had heard Anna correctly. He needed to confirm what he thought she had said.

'You mean there could be a job for me with the Mustermanns, when you leave?' he asked.

'Not could be, there will be,' Anna replied. 'They will need someone to be responsible for the finances of the Mustermann Corporation. I have told them about you. Now they want to meet you. See if you would fit in.'

'I really don't know what to say, is my immediate response. I will have to consider this very carefully. Besides, my wife is going through a difficult time at present. She is under great pressure at work. I can't just walk out and leave her to cope on her own. It would be out of the question to take her with me'

Anna nodded to indicate she understood. She continued, 'What I am bringing you is a proposal from the Mustermann Corporation with an offer to become Director of Finance. I am not offering you a proposal of marriage!' David hadn't thought for one minute that Anna's proposal had anything to do with marriage.

She continued, 'It is easy to get to Stuttgart. You can fly from London Gatwick. Someone will pick you up from the airport, probably Franz.'

Oh no, thought David, but he said nothing.

'You will meet Klaus and Sophia. They are lovely people. You can play tennis and chess against Franz. He is excellent at both.'

David frowned.

'I will have to let you know. Remember what I said about Emma. I need to support her at the moment.'

Emma was coming under increasing pressure at work. One day, unexpectedly, her own GP, Dr Brown, visited her in her office. He began with trivial chit-chat about the family, and about David in particular. She said nothing about her deteriorating relationship with David.

'I and other members of staff are becoming more and more concerned about you,' said Dr Brown. 'Over the past few months you seem to have gone from being a happy and efficient Practice Manager to one who is struggling to do the job. Do you think that's a fair comment?'

Emma played with the pen on her desk before answering. 'I'm not finding the job as easy or fulfilling as I once did.'

'Are there reasons why you think this may be the case?'

Emma replied immediately, 'I'm trying to do my own job, plus all I have taken on from Dr Thompson.' Dr Thompson was the CEO of the Trust, until he went off sick with stress.

'You had your holiday last month. 'Was everything OK before that?'

'Yes, reasonably OK. It was just before my

holiday that Dr Thompson went off sick,' Emma explained.

'And were there any differences when you returned from holiday?'

'Oh yes. Things didn't seem the same,' Emma said. 'I found it difficult to fit back in. Rotas and schedules had changed. I felt like an outsider.'

'What about the events during your holiday?' Dr Brown enquired. 'Did they cause difficulties?'

'Patients and some staff who don't know me were quick to point a finger. I found the first day back a terrible ordeal on top of the extra work.' Emma felt the pressure of the doctor's questions beginning to tell on her. Dr Brown thought there were certain questions that need to be asked concerning some of the gossip that had come to his ears. It may only be hearsay, so he had to tread very carefully, but he had to ask the questions anyway.

'Was your husband able to support you in all of this?'

'Not really,' Emma said. 'We've hardly spoken about it. Things were not easy before going on holiday. Then he went off with another woman.'

Dr Brown was shocked by this latest revelation. He had heard stories about difficulties in the marriage, but this took things to a new level.

'Your husband actually went off with another woman while you were on holiday?'

'He spent more time with her than with me.'

'So has he seen her since you've been home?'

'No,' Emma replied. Then after a pause she said, 'She's German. Hopefully she's in Germany.'

Dr Brown took the conversation down the reconciliation route.

'There are several sources of help and support for couples struggling with marriage problems, as you well know. I have known you and Mr Burrows since I joined the practice twenty years ago. I could meet with you both and see how we could move things forward. Or you might like to try a Marriage Guidance Counsellor.'

Emma remained silent for a while.

'I don't think any of that would work. David refuses to talk about our marriage. He doesn't think there is anything wrong. When I raise the subject, he looks glum and won't talk.'

Dr Brown decided to change tack. He would raise the subject he had in mind when he came to see Emma.

'You have a lot going on at work and in your private life. I think you should seriously consider taking a break. What do you say?'

'I'm not sure.'

'You can't go on like this,' said the doctor. 'It could lead to you having a complete breakdown, or making a mistake which will be costly to the Trust.' Dr Brown's words had been carefully chosen and did have the desired impact on Emma.

'I'll think about it.'

'Do consider it carefully,' said Dr Brown, as he stood up. 'Do try and bring yourself to talk it over with Mr Burrows.' With that, he left Emma's office. David would be the last person she would want to talk with about her increasing problems at work. One of the girls would be far more understanding.

Emma arrived home from work first. She decided to make a casserole for dinner. David liked casserole and there was plenty of time to get it ready. David picked up the aroma as soon as he walked in through the front door.

'Something smells good,' he said.

'Casserole. Would you like a glass of wine with it?' She thought this might open the way for them to discuss their marriage.

'Yes, why not? I'm not out tonight.'

Emma felt she needed to get the talking going right away, if they were ever to get talking about their marital problems before the end of the meal. She launched in by asking David to speak about his work, a subject about which he was never lost for words.

'Has everything returned to normal after the inspection? And after your interview?'

David thought they were going to talk about their marriage. He was rather taken aback and annoyed by Emma's question.

'Things are certainly not back to normal,' he said. 'There's more red tape, to make sure it doesn't happen again.'

'I'm sure you can cope with that. It happened in your department, but you were on holiday. They can't blame you.'

'That's just the point. I am getting blamed. There was nothing I could do as I was on holiday in France. Brian has changed. He now calls me Mr Burrows. He came in and lectured me the other day. I'm being made the scapegoat for what went wrong. I wonder how long I have left at IFS.' David finished on this pessimistic note to prepare Emma if he lost his job in the near future.

'I'm sorry to hear that. I thought you would have taken it in your stride. I'm surprised Brian has become a turncoat.'

'So what about you,' David asked.

'Well, as you know, it wasn't easy going back to work, with slurs flying around like no one's business. There have been changes. I'm feeling under pressure to do more than just my job.'

'How come?'

'The CEO went off with stress just before we went on holiday. When I came back, I found I had been given some of what Dr Thompson did as CEO.'

'Can't you just tell somebody you can't cope with any more work?'

'I don't know. It doesn't work like that. Our doctor came in to see me today.'

'What, Dr Brown?'

'Yes. He said he was concerned I'm not coping.'

'What did you think of that?'

'I'm not coping at present.'

'Did Dr Brown come up with any ideas to relieve the stress you're working under?'

'Of course not. He just pointed out there was a problem. He didn't come up with any solutions.'

'What do you think would help?'

'Less work,' said Emma in a flash.

'Do you mean going part-time?'

'Possibly, or taking a complete break from work.' Emma suggested this as though she had just thought of it.

'How do you go about doing part-time, or having

a break?'

'I expect I'll have to put it to the board. Dr Brown would be in favour, I'm sure. If I go and convince him and then let him think it's his idea, he will then convince the powers that be.'

David clapped his hands together.

'That's alright then, it's as good as sorted! I was going to ask how I could be involved in helping to relieve the pressure on you.'

'That's very sweet of you,' Emma said, 'but I can manage. I don't need your help.'

'I thought one of the duties of a loving husband was to protect and support his wife.' As he said this, he realised there could be lots of extra work coming in his direction if Emma took up his offer. He ought not to make rash promises which he might live to regret later.

When Emma spoke, what she said amazed David.

'It's always good to know we have a strong marriage. I know I can call on you whenever I need you. No! I don't need any help at the moment.'

David could hardly believe his ears. Over recent weeks he and Emma had come to accept there were problems with their marriage. They had frequently been at loggerheads. Now Emma was saying their marriage was cast iron. There was no need for remedial action. David knew Emma was in denial. This made things much more difficult. There was no point in having a slanging match. He changed the course of the conversation to let Emma know the seriousness of the situation at International Financial Services.

'You know I said there was a breakdown in relationship between me and Brian. 'I flippantly talked about leaving IFS. Well, there is an encouraging development. I have had a message from the Mustermann family. I could be appointed Director of Finance for the family business. Emma showed no response, favourable or otherwise, to what David said. He continued speaking about this new opportunity.

'I will have to go to Germany sometime, to find out more; to see if they like me.'

Emma smiled. 'Of course they'll like you,' she said.

'Then, if I get the job,' David said, 'We will have to move to Germany.'

Emma left a long silence before she replied.

'What you're saying is that we will have to move to Germany or live apart. That would be fine whatever happens. I'm sure we'll manage.'

David was again surprised at Emma's reaction to what he'd told her. In for a penny, in for a pound, he thought.

'The Mustermann Corporation would like to see me. Perhaps next week. As soon as it can be arranged.'

'That's OK. I hope you get the job,' Emma said, as she started clearing the table. David knew he would have to continue this conversation later, much later. Emma just didn't seem to grasp the enormity of what he had told her.

Later that night David gave Sue a ring. 'Hi Sue!'

'Hello daddy! Good to hear from you. How are you?'

'OK. There's a lot going on at the moment.'

'Such as?' Sue asked.

'There was a problem at work while we were

on holiday' David explained. 'We all had to be interviewed. It was soon sorted. The top brass have brought in new rules. Things aren't the same any more. My manager treats me like dirt. I did tell him my days at IFS were probably numbered.

'Steady on! It's not wise to leave a job at present. You never know when you'll get another.'

'It's OK. I won't leave without having something else lined up.'

'I'm glad to hear that. So how's mum?' Sue asked.

'She's the main reason I'm ringing,' David said. 'She's having a tough time. She found it difficult to live down all the talk about what happened on holiday. Me going off with another woman! I told you what happened.'

'Yes, but I can understand that it hurt. Even if it wasn't true.'

'But she keeps on making out I am in a relationship with Anna. Like she did when we came over to see you. Now she's under great pressure at work and can't cope. Even our doctor's noticed she's struggling. She doesn't want any help from him. Nor from me. Says she can cope.'

'Oh Mum, why do you do it?' said Sue. 'Why does she go on pretending things are fine when they aren't?'

'The worst of it is she thinks our marriage is fine and will weather the storm.'

'From what you've said to me in the past, there have been problems.'

'Yes, but then she accepted they existed,' David said. 'Not now. If things don't improve, I'll go and see

Dr Brown. I thought you ought to know about this, darling.'

'Yes, thanks for telling me. Do keep me informed. Bye, Dad.' With that she rang off, leaving David to wonder what his next move should be.

A few days later David had a text from Anna, 'How RU? I'm inviting you to meet the Mustermanns in a week's time in Stuttgart. RSVP. A.'

David replied, 'Working on it.' He would have to mention this to Emma and give Sue and Pat a ring.

After dinner, David felt the time was right, as he and Emma drank coffee.

'You remember I said I thought the bosses at IFS were trying to get rid of me. And that I might get a job in Germany. I've had an invitation to go there for a few days next week.'

'That will be OK then,' Emma commented. 'When will you go?'

'Thursday 11th in the afternoon. Come back Sunday or Monday. 'I've already booked next week off as I was going to Normandy with Paul.'

'That's good,' Emma said. David was becoming increasingly convinced that Emma didn't understand what he was saying. He would go and see Dr Brown about Emma's deteriorating mental state. He could also tell him about his trip to Germany. David was uncertain about what else he should say to Emma. So far her response seemed to indicate complete indifference. He did give Sue and Pat a ring, to keep them informed. Both said they would make sure Emma was well looked after while he was away.

14

DECISIONS! DECISIONS!

The next day David went to see Brian, his manager.

'I have already booked 8th to 12th September off for a holiday,' he said. 'Would it now be alright if I work on Monday 8th, so I can have Monday 15th off? It's just that I've been invited to do something for the weekend and I can then travel back on Monday.'

Brian nodded.

'That will be fine,' he said as he changed David's holiday dates on the online system. 'Are you doing anything nice?'

'It's a private function, so I'm not at liberty to say.' David thought perhaps that would shut him up!

Later David sent a text to Anna, confirming that he would be in Stuttgart 11th to 15th September. As soon as he had sent it, he remembered he wanted to meet her before going to Stuttgart, so he could talk over the arrangements. He was still cursing himself for leaving this off the text when his mobile rang. It was Anna.

'Thank you for agreeing to come to Stuttgart.'

'That's alright. Where are you going to be over the next few days? Monday 8th in particular? I'm working that day; then off for the rest of the week. Could we meet for an evening meal on 8th? I need to ask you about the trip.'

'We could meet at the restaurant in Charing Cross at 7 o'clock,' she suggested.

'That's excellent,' David said, as Emma breezed into the lounge.

'What is,' she asked.

'I've planned to meet a colleague after work next Monday.'

'Did you ask my permission?' Emma asked.

'I didn't know I had to,' David replied.

'It would have been courteous to have done so. But you thought I might say, 'No,' so you didn't bother to ask.' David fell silent, taken aback by what Emma had said. She picked up her book.

'I'm heading to bed. I've had a tiring day.' He listened to her footsteps picking out the occasional squeaky floor boards on the stairs.

On the Monday David kept thinking about seeing Anna again. The prospect of meeting her brightened up an otherwise lack-lustre day. As he tidied his desk he realised he would not be back in the office for another week. It was just like going on holiday. He was going on holiday, to Germany for a few days, with the prospect of getting a new job thrown in. Germany was a country he knew little about. His mind then went back to the last time he closed up the office several weeks ago, prior to setting off for Normandy. He would appreciate a less eventful trip this time. He thought it wise to take a look at every part of the office. Everything looked in order, so he picked up his case and left. Sarah wasn't in reception to bid him farewell this time.

Anna was at the restaurant waiting for him. She's keen, he thought. They embraced briefly. Her kiss was passionate.

'It is lovely to see you again,' she said.

'And to see you. Tell me, what do I need to know about my trip to Stuttgart?'

'You are booked on the flight from London Gatwick to Stuttgart on Thursday departing at 1600. Here is your ticket.'

David was surprised that Anna handed him his ticket. He took a quick glance and noticed he was flying British Airways.

'It's a good airline,' he commented.

'I think so,' Anna added.

'How much do I owe?'

'Nothing. It has been paid for by the family.'

'They must think it's worth flying me over from the UK.'

'They know all about you from what I have told them. They said they would pay your air fare to Stuttgart. It is only a single ticket!' she said jokingly.

'When I get to Stuttgart, what do I do?' asked David.

'Someone will be there to meet you,' said Anna.

'And what about you? Will you be at the airport?'

'I will see you at Stuttgart airport.'

'That's good to know,' he said. 'At least there will be one person I've met before and who can speak

English!' The arrival of the food restricted their conversation, but David still had a number of questions to ask.

'What are you doing for the rest of this week?'

'I will spend part of the time in London, sorting out the details of my contract,' Anna said. 'I also need to be in Stuttgart, working on my final company report and financial statement.'

'Can you tell me what's going to happen over the weekend? Am I going to be formally interviewed?'

'I am sure there will be some sort of discussion with Klaus and Franz. You will also get a chance to see Stuttgart.'

'That will be good,' David said, 'So it's not all formal discussions and interviews! Did you tell Franz that I am no good at tennis or chess?'

'Yes I did. Franz said it was such a pity. He was looking forward to beating you.'

As they were having coffee Anna said, 'I must be going soon. I have a lot to do. It is OK for you being on holiday!'

'I am also very busy. I need to make sure Emma will be alright. If she throws a wobbly while I'm away, I need to know that there will be someone to pick up the pieces.'

'What is a wobbly?' she asked.

'When Emma is not well physically or mentally and can't cope with life on her own. That's what I call a wobbly.'

Anna picked up her handbag and got up to leave. She kissed David.

'I will see you on Thursday.'

'Yes, I look forward to that,' David replied.

She then strode purposefully out of the restaurant having accomplished her mission.

When David arrived home Emma was in the lounge doing some embroidery, with Beethoven's Pastoral Symphony in the background. 'I do like that music,' he said. 'It brings to mind beautiful countryside views and a great feeling of peace.'

'Hmm,' Emma responded, reluctant to agree.

'What sort of day have you had?' asked David.

'It's been alright. I was terribly busy all morning, so the time went quickly. How about you?'

'Average. At least I'm on holiday now till Tuesday of next week.'

'How was your meal with your friend tonight?'

'Good.'

'Anyone I know?' Emma asked.

'No. Just a friend.'

'What are you going to do tomorrow and Wednesday, before you go to Germany?'

'I thought I'd have a game of golf, probably Wednesday,' David said. 'I also need to book up Gatwick Parking and pack sometime. I'm sure I'll find plenty to do.'

'The lawns for instance,' Emma said pleadingly.

'Yes the lawns too. I think I will go and make a coffee and go to bed early,' he said. 'It's been a long day.' He made a coffee and took it upstairs.

By the time Emma went to bed, David was fast asleep and snoring loudly. His full mug of coffee was still on the bedside cabinet.

David knew he would have to show considerable tact and diplomacy in making an appointment to see

Dr Brown. He rang early in the day and asked for the doctor to ring him back at the end of the morning when he had finished his surgery. He arranged to go and see him early the next morning.

At lunch time David took himself off to the Chafford Arms. Few of his drinking friends were there, but it was good to relax and have a chat. One of the issues that came up in conversation was the way Emma had reacted to the events during the holiday in Normandy and the damaging impact this had made on her life.

David had a passing acquaintance with a number of the men. They were older than him and he thought they had all retired. They spoke wise words, born out of life's experiences.

'One thing you can't predict is how something that seems so trivial is going to impact a person's life,' Bert said,

Charlie told them that one person will react to a tragedy in one way, but someone else will behave completely differently.

'My brother and sister-in-law lost a child when they were in their twenties. Other children came along and my brother has been happy-go-lucky just like he always was. His wife has never recovered from the loss.'

Will asked David a question.

'You've managed to stay calm through all that happened, but your wife hasn't. Does she speak about it much?'

David shook his head. 'Sadly not. I wish she would.'

Charlie offered another nugget of wisdom.

'It's not possible to know what's going on in that sweet little head of hers,' he said with a sad look on his face. As they went their separate ways, these men wished David good luck in encouraging Emma back to full physical and mental health. Despite their wisdom, David had to accept that he had to cope with the situation on his own.

The next day David was up and out early. He parked up and walked to the surgery. The place had changed since his last visit several years ago. The electronic patient call-in board was just one indication that it had moved into the twenty-first century. He had a few minutes to browse some of the gardening magazines before he was called.

Dr. Brown stood waiting for David outside his consulting room.

'Good morning Mr Burrows,' he said as he shook David's hand. 'Come in and have a seat. It's a long time since your last appointment with me.'

'Yes. I notice a greater use of modern technology since the last time I was here.'

'So how can I help you?'

'Several years ago I used to attend the Well Man Clinic,' said David. 'I've not been for a number of years. I thought it was time I had an MOT and service.'

Dr. Brown looked at his screen and said, 'The last time was in 2004. We no longer do that. Everyone between forty and seventy-four is now urged to have an NHS health check. It's similar to the Well Man Clinic. You will be asked a few questions about your health. Your blood pressure will be checked and you will have a blood test. You will also be weighed. You will need to bring with you a sample of urine to be tested. All this will be done by a nurse. You can book up for an NHS health check at reception when you leave.'

'OK, I'll do that. That's it for me,' said David. 'I also wanted to have a word with you about Emma. She's found it difficult to hold things together since coming back from holiday. She's struggling and I don't know what to do to help. Emma says she doesn't need my help and she will be alright to cope on her own. A few weeks ago we both had to admit that our marriage wasn't as good as it could be. Recently she said we had a strong marriage! She's confused. I think she wants to pretend that our marriage is as strong as it was years ago.'

Dr. Brown was thoughtful for a moment.

'I think perhaps my idea of her taking a break would be good.'

David raised his eyebrows.

'She was going to bring that to you as her idea.'

'I see,' said the doctor.

David thought he should reveal some of the difficulties he was having at work.

'It looks as if I may be made redundant at any time. I do have the opportunity of becoming Financial Director for a large corporation in Germany.'

Now it was time for Dr. Brown to show surprise.

'I wonder if that's wise bearing in mind your wife's present state of health.'

'I have talked it over with Emma over the last few days,' David said. 'She says she's OK with it. I'm going there on Thursday for a long weekend, to find out more about the job. My daughter, Sue, and Emma's friend, Pat, will make sure Emma is alright while I'm away.'

Dr. Brown ran his hand over his chin. He was reviewing all he had heard about David and Emma.

'Leave it to me,' he said. 'I'll see what can be done. I'll try to relieve a lot of the pressure on Emma at work.' With that he stood up and said. 'Thank you for coming in and putting me in the picture. Don't forget to book up an NHS health check on your way out.'

David walked slowly towards the exit, thinking over all that had been discussed. He realised things were worse than he'd thought and he knew he was as much to blame as Emma.

David woke up early on Thursday, the day he was to fly to Stuttgart. He showered, got dressed and went downstairs. Emma was still finishing her mug of tea.

'Today's the day I'm off to Germany,' he said.

'I have remembered. Something about you going for a job.'

'Yes, that's it.'

'If you get the job we'll need to work out where to live, in Germany or in England.'

'I haven't got the job yet!' David said cautiously. 'Don't worry your head about where we'll live in the future. Just live for today.'

Emma put her breakfast washing up in the sink.

'I'll do that,' he said. 'You get off to work and have a good day.'

It wasn't long before Emma came downstairs and picked up her jacket and brief case.

'Do have a lovely time,' she said.

'I'll try and ring you each evening if I can,' he said. Following this brief exchange, Emma walked along the hall and out of the front door.

David dutifully did the washing up and left it to drain. He wandered into the garden contemplating what he might do. Although it was cloudy, it wasn't cold. The lawns would have to wait until his return. Armed with a pair of secateurs and a large plastic sack, he continued cutting back shrubs he began doing a few weeks back. He had intended going in for coffee mid-morning, but the time had flown by and he went in for an early lunch. He put a few items of clothing into a small case. It suddenly occurred to him that he had forgotten to buy a present. Not that the Mustermanns needed any presents by all accounts. It would be good to take something that typified England. Emma was the one who came up with good ideas on such occasions, but in the state she was in, she hadn't given it another thought. She would often buy chocolates or drink. Chocolates might not be appropriate and anything alcoholic would be like carrying coals to Newcastle. He would see if he could pick up something in the airport shops, probably something tacky with a Union Jack on it.

David was relieved that the check-in experience went smoothly. He was a little concerned that his ticket may not be valid. Stories often circulated about passengers who had been given tickets by a friend and they turned out to be fakes. He trusted Anna and this trust was well-founded. The check-in operator was a young lady with short blonde hair. She asked David if he had packed his case himself.

'If it has to be opened, you will see that only I could pack it like that!' He winked and said, 'That's a 'yes' then!' He bought a coffee and a pastry. Then he spent a long time looking for a suitable present. He eventually bought some Scottish shortbread biscuits, thinking to himself that Scotland was still part of the UK. The referendum vote the following week confirmed the status quo. He also purchased a calendar depicting London landmarks and a magazine to read. It only took slightly longer to go through security, in spite of the extra measures that had been introduced over recent weeks. He relaxed and began reading his magazine. He was looking forward to the next four days.

15

GERMAN EXPERIENCE

W hen the flight was called David took his place in the queue to board. He walked down the aisle to find his seat. When he reached it he was greeted by a cheery voice.

'Hello David!' It was Anna.

'I might have known,' he said. 'How did I not see you before?'

'Because you are not observant enough!' Anna said, holding out her hands and shrugging her shoulders.

Devious lady, he thought. No, not devious, mysterious.

'It's good to have you to travel with me,' David said. 'It seems to make the time go so much quicker.'

'But we both know that the flight will take the same time as it would if you travelled alone!'

'Did you manage to sort out your contract in London?' David asked.

'Yes, that's all fine.'

'Did you fly to Germany to complete paperwork for the Mustermanns?'

'No. The contract took longer to agree than I thought it would. There was much discussion on some parts. There was not enough time to go to Stuttgart and then be back at Gatwick to fly with you.'

'Why did you want to fly with me?' David asked.

'I thought it would be nice,' Anna said. Then she added, 'It shows my concern for your needs,' and she squeezed his arm.

He didn't reply. He was uncertain what she meant, so he changed the subject.

'Will there be some official welcome?' What about the evening meal?'

'It is likely to be informal,' she said.

'What sort of clothes should I wear?'

'Smart casual is the term you would use,' she replied.

'Will there be formal speeches?' David asked, with a look of concern on his face.

'No,' Anna said, patting the back of his hand. 'You will be able to cope with anything that comes your way.'

As good as it was having Anna beside him on the flight, David longed for silence, to have time to himself just to read his magazine. It would be rude to start reading, he thought, when maybe she wanted to talk. After all, Anna had done so much to make sure she would travel with him. Once airborne, David looked across at Anna. Her head was back and she was fast asleep. He could now enjoy the peace for which he longed.

It was a smooth flight and there was only a slight

delay going through security. David and Anna walked from the terminal into fading daylight.

'Have you visited Stuttgart before?' asked Anna.

'No.'

'You should make a wish then.'

Anna soon located the BMW in the car park and David was introduced to Franz.

'I've heard a lot about you, but I've never met you before,' David said.

'Yes,' said Franz. 'I am disappointed you will not play me at tennis or chess. Oh! I am sorry I damaged your car.' Franz spoke with a German accent, but David found his English easy to understand.

'You sit in the front, David.' said Anna. 'Your case can come in the back with me.'

After a lengthy journey they reached the castle. Anna got out first and then opened the front passenger door, so David was able to step down from the vehicle. A large wooden door opened at the front of the castle. A couple emerged and walked towards the BMW.

Anna led David forward and introduced him.

'Herr und Frau Mustermann, Das ist Herr David Burrows.' David stepped forward and shook hands.

Herr Mustermann said, 'Ich hoffe, dass Sie Ihren Aufenthalt bei uns genießen und Stuttgart reizvoll finden.'

Anna translated, 'I hope you will enjoy your stay with us and you will find Stuttgart a charming city.' Herr Mustermann led the way into the castle, leaving Franz to park the car and bring in the luggage. Once inside, Herr Mustermann continued, 'Ich freue mich, dass Sie die Einladung mit der Familie Mustermann das

Wochenende zu verbringen, angenommen haben.'

'I am glad you accepted the invitation to spend the weekend with the Mustermann family.'

He completed his words of welcome, 'Ich gehe davon aus, dass Sie gekommen sind, um über die Möglichkeit zu sprechen, das Sie den Stelle des Finanzdirektors in dem Mustermann-Imperium übernehmen'

'I understand you have come to talk over the possibility of becoming Director of Finance for the Mustermann Empire.'

David thanked Herr Mustermann for making it possible for him to travel to Germany. He said he was very grateful for the opportunity to work for such an important family business. Herr Mustermann replied, saying there would be plenty of time to discuss business later. In the meantime he told David to enjoy himself.

Franz picked up David's bag and quickly set off up the stairs, to show him to his room. David followed at a more leisurely pace. Franz opened the door and dropped the case inside. Then he set off running and passed David on the stairs.

Sometime later Anna and David descended to the hallway, looking brighter and fresher. Herr Mustermann invited David to have a glass of wine. David was uncertain quite what to do. He bowed his head and took a sip of some exceedingly fine wine. Fortunately Anna was on hand the next time Herr Mustermann spoke to David.

Frau Mustermann came in and invited everyone to take their seats at the table. A truly splendid meal was set before them. David was sitting next to Franz and he spent much of the meal talking to him about his university education, as well as sport and art. Anna was sitting with the senior members of the family. David knew so few words of German that he was unable to follow the conversation. However, from their body language and facial expressions he thought it was a very serious discussion. Coffee was served in the lounge at the end of the meal.

At breakfast the next morning Anna briefed David on the plans for the day.

'This morning Franz, you and I will go on a tour of the Mercedes-Benz museum. After that there will be an opportunity to discover some of the sights of Stuttgart. You will have a chance to buy a drink at Biddy Early's Irish Pub where everyone speaks English.

'That sounds good to me,' he said. 'I look forward to it.'

'At sometime during the afternoon or evening,' she said, Herr Mustermann would like to talk with you about the job he is offering. I will, of course, act as interpreter for that meeting.'

David found the Mercedes-Benz museum a truly fascinating experience. The tour, punctuated by stops for coffee, took in the history of the brand and its iconic three-pointed star trademark. He was reminded about many of the Mercedes classic and racing car designs. He looked with envy at some of the current models. He expressed his enthusiasm to Anna.

'This museum has been brilliantly designed. I think it's excellent. Perhaps I will treat myself to a Mercedes if I work for the Mustermann family.'

They strolled around Stuttgart, ending up in Biddy Early's Irish Pub, where they stopped for something to eat, washed down with a pint of Guinness. David struck up conversation with one of the barmen and he found out that a Celtic band would be playing that night. Anna said, 'I'm sure Herr Mustermann will do your interview this afternoon, so we can come back here tonight.'

'That would be good,' he said.

Later that afternoon Anna appeared in the lounge doorway and said, 'Mr Burrows, Herr Mustermann will see you now.' He got up from the sofa and tried to shake off the tiredness he had experienced over the past few minutes. He followed Anna along a corridor decorated with photographs and paintings of mountain scenery. They entered a wooden panelled room of considerable proportions. There were also photographs exhibited here. David assumed they were family members. The modern ones were in colour, but some were in black and white and a few in sepia. Herr Mustermann was seated at the far end of the room and gestured for David to join him. As he approached, Herr Mustermann spoke to Anna, presumably to ask her to tell David about the people in the photographs.

'This is Max Mustermann and his wife, Irmgard Hertzog,' Anna began. 'They were born in the 1920's. He is the first Max Mustermann, who started the Mustermann Corporation.' Nearby were other black and white photos, darker and more difficult to see the figures clearly. David thought these were probably parents or siblings of Max or Irmgard, but not sufficiently important to get a mention from Anna. 'This is their son, also called Max, who married Birgit.' David thought it a bit strange that Anna gave her no second name. There was no time to dwell on this as Anna had moved on. She announced the next names as Klaus Mustermann and Sophia Schmidt whom he recognised as his host and hostess. This was the first photo to be in colour. Around the photograph of Klaus and Sophia were a number of smaller photos, one showing a baby in arms. Another was a photo of Sophia sitting on a lawn with two children playing in front of her. The boy looked like Franz. The girl was older. More questions occurred to David, but he dared not articulate them. Finally there were some photos of Franz, taken when he was in his teens. One showed him with a group of swimmers, another in which he was holding a rifle and a third when he was dressed for skiing.

As Anna and David walked to join Herr Mustermann, he was rearranging chairs for them. He began by giving details of the job and the credentials he expected from the person appointed to be Director of Finance.

'Sie erkennen die Größe und Bedeutung der Kapitalgesellschaft Mustermann,' he said. 'Der Finanz-direktor ist für alle Transaktionen von der Gesellschaft vorgenommen verantwortlich. Er oder sie wird in der Gegenwart und Franz beantwortbar zu mir in den kommenden Jahren.'

'You realise the size and importance of the Mustermann business corporation,' Anna said. 'The financial director is responsible for all the transactions undertaken by the corporation. He or she will be answerable to me at present and to Franz in the years ahead.'

'Anna hat mir gesagt wie effizient Sie in Ihrem derzeitigen Job sind,' sagte Herr Mustermann.

'Anna told me how efficient you are in your current job,' said Herr Mustermann

This took David by surprise. How could she know about his competence or otherwise at IFS? Perhaps she knew more about what went on there than she had let on.

'Sie werden alle Ihre finanziellen Fähigkeiten für mich arbeiten müssen,' uhr er fort. 'Ich suche jemanden, der Anna zu ersetzen und nehmen die Finanzen auf eine neue Ebene der Kompetenz.'

'You will need all your financial skills to work for me,' he said through Anna. 'I am looking for someone to replace Anna and take the finances to a new level of competence.'

'After a lengthy pause, he spoke to Anna. She then looked at David with a quizzical expression on her face and said, 'Glauben Sie, Sie sind der Mann?'

'Do you think you are the man?'

'Yes, I think I am!' David said.

She communicated this to Herr Mustermann. He got up from his chair and shook David firmly by the hand. Returning to his seat, he went through some details of the contract.

'Ich schlage vor, Sie werden 100.000 € für die ersten sechs Monate gezahlt werden. Während dieser Zeit wird es einen Monat im Voraus für Sie und für mich. Am Ende der 6 Monate werden Sie 250.000 € pro Jahr bezahlt werden. Was sagen Sie?'

'I am suggesting you will be paid 100,000euros for the first six months. During that time there will one month's notice for you and for me. At the end of six months you will be paid 250,000euros per annum. What do you say?'

David got up from his seat and shook hands with Herr Mustermann. 'I agree, 'he said.

Herr Mustermann then proceeded to speak with Anna at length. It all sounded high-powered and technical to David. Finally Herr Mustermann smiled as Anna looked at David and said, 'Herr Mustermann wondered if £5,000 was sufficient for the repair of your car?'

David hardly knew what to say. It wasn't a question he was expecting. He nodded and said, 'Yes.' He stood up and shook hands once again and took his leave.

After the interview it was back to Stuttgart and the Irish pub. David felt it was a celebration party laid on for his benefit. He had a great time drinking and listening to the music. He managed to strike up conversations with several people, most of whom were female. He seemed to attract them as a magnet attracts iron. It really was a friendly pub and he had been blessed by the experience. What a great way to end a great day, during which he had landed himself another job.

Next morning Franz did the briefing for David's benefit. 'We will visit Esslingen am Neckar. You will see parts of this city and we will tell you about its history. We will also have a walk in the mountains. There will be a lunch of sandwiches, which Anna has prepared'

'It sounds great,' said David. 'I can't wait to get started.'

Esslingen am Neckar lived up to the billing Franz had given it. David was in awe and wonder, as he walked around the cobbled streets, gazing at buildings which spanned a thousand years. It was the kind of enchanting place that he and Emma used to visit in England and abroad. Sadly she had recently lost interest. Now as soon as they arrived, Emma would get bored and want to move on to somewhere else. Anna and Franz did an excellent job describing the history of Esslingen am Neckar.

Anna had prepared a feast for lunch, consisting of sandwiches, salad and fresh fruit, together with a bottle of dry white wine. Once again David marvelled at the beauty which surrounded them.

'What magnificent scenery,' he exclaimed. He thought how fortunate he had been to encounter scenes like this when he was ostensibly there for a job interview.

'Tomorrow we could go to Europa-Park,' said Franz, 'if you feel up to it.' David realised Franz was looking at him when he said this. He was calling into question his ability to withstand a day out at a theme park. 'There is a large choice of rides,' Franz continued, 'roller coaster and water rides.'

In spite of being thirty years older, David had to accept the challenge. 'I'm up for that he said.'

After lunch they went on a walk around the hills, Franz leading the way. It was as if he was laying down a challenge for tomorrow. David and Anna walked along some distance behind, engaged in frivolous chit-chat.

Once back at the castle they had a shower and changed, ready for the meal. Anna appeared wearing a brightly- coloured dress, which in David's eyes, made her look even more attractive. There was no sign of Franz's parents. The three of them dined alone. After the meal each of them resorted to reading. It wasn't long before they drank coffee and retired to bed early.

At breakfast Franz and David were wearing sports shirts showing allegiance to their homeland. 'It will take us two hours to get to Europa-Park,' Franz said. 'Then we can enjoy the rides.' Although the rivalry was between David and Franz, Anna also joined in and went on the same rides. Each of them got wet or very wet on the rides, but they soon dried out. By the end of their stay they felt battered and bruised and somewhat nauseous, but nobody had refused to go on any ride. They shook hands with each other and David gave Anna a peck on the cheek.

That evening Klaus and Sophia joined the others for dinner. The conversation was mainly about the rides Anna, David and Franz had experienced at Europa-Park. Klaus and Sophia listened with interest. David thought he should express his gratitude, as this was the last time they would all be together. 'I am so grateful for your welcome and the hospitality you have shown to me over the past few days. It has been a wonderful experience for me in a part of the world I have never visited before. Thank you very much. He left Anna to pass on his sentiments to his hosts.

Next morning Anna and David had an early breakfast. 'I will be driving you to the airport,' Anna said.

'Are you not coming back to England with me?' David asked.

'I have a number of things to complete here. I will catch up with you in London,' she said reassuringly.

'I look forward to that.'

Herr Mustermann came to say farewell. He gave David an envelope. Anna read a prepared script, 'In the envelope is a summary of the discussions you had with Herr Mustermann concerning the job,' she said, 'including details of the salary. Herr Mustermann would like you to study these papers and then put in writing your acceptance of the offer to be the Director of Finance for the Mustermann Corporation. He would appreciate you doing this as soon as possible.'

'I will do it as soon as I can,' David said through Anna. 'Please bear in mind that I have to give notice to my current employer.'

After a brief conversation with her boss, Anna said, 'Herr Mustermann understands.' He stepped forward and shook hands with David.

Anna put David's case in the back of the BMW and after they had both climbed aboard, she drove confidently away. There was an uneasy silence on the way to the airport. David was experiencing a mixture of emotions. It was good that he had been offered another job. The interview, if that's what it was, must have gone well. It was good to have spent the last four days with Anna, but there was little chance for them to be together on their own. The chemistry between them had no chance to develop. Perhaps that was the way Anna wanted it; a business relationship and mutual admiration for one another, but nothing more.

'You are deep in thought,' Anna said. 'What are you thinking about?'

'I'm sad you are not coming back with me,' he replied. 'It's not going to be easy giving in my notice at IFS. Also I have to tell Emma what's happening.'

'Will you expect Emma to come and live in Germany when you start work here?'

'I don't think she would,' David replied, 'but I still have to keep her informed. Then she can make up her own mind, whether to stay in the UK or not, with a little guidance from me.' Anna wasn't convinced but remained silent. 'When are you going to be back in London?' David asked her.

'Maybe by the end of this week, or sometime next week. I will let you know how things are going.'

'Do you realise how much I want to be with you?' David asked. 'Just being with you has helped me through the difficulties of the past few weeks, coping with Emma and offering me help to get another job.' There was another long period of silence, broken by Anna.

'All will turn out right in the end,' she said.

At the airport David moved to give Anna a hug and a kiss. She offered only her cheek and moved away as soon as he had kissed it. He couldn't understand Anna's apparent lack of passion. All he managed to say was, 'I look forward to hearing from you.'

'Yes, OK, I will be in touch.'

Doubts flooded into his mind. Had he read more into the relationship than Anna intended? Was she getting cold feet? David was disgruntled to say the least. He grabbed the handle of his case and strode off determinedly towards the terminal.

16

CHANGING TIMES

David enjoyed a pleasant journey back to Penshurst. There was time to remember what had happened during his visit to Stuttgart. It had been good, with some exceptional occasions. But what should he make of Anna's attitude at the airport? He should be pleased that she had helped him obtain a job, but did he want it? Of course he did. It would be stupid to turn it down. But he knew the job would have its problems, working in Europe for an employer who wasn't English. And if Anna's heart had now grown cold, one of the main attractions of working in Stuttgart would no longer exist. Perhaps this was the reason behind Anna's determination to get a job in London. Perhaps this was the way she had planned it all along. In the midst of all these thoughts David realised he had forgotten to phone Emma over the weekend, not just one night but all four nights. There was nothing he could do about that now, except grovel and apologise when he met up with her.

At home David continued his thinking while

ambling around the garden. It was a pleasant day, but he didn't fancy doing any gardening. He eventually took himself inside and prepared something to eat. He did the best he could from a fridge that had little to offer.

As he ate he turned the pages of the national daily on the table. After his meal he gave his attention to the small pile of post. There was the usual amount of junk mail, plus a bill from Baileys and a bank statement for their joint account. He scrutinised this and thought the balance was about right. He would check this against receipts later.

Then he opened the envelope from Herr Mustermann, spreading out the contents in front of him. It was a very full set of documents and he assumed these had been typed up by Anna. He read each page carefully. One was a job description. Another gave the terms and conditions of his employment, including his salary. When he came to the sheet he had to sign, he read each line twice over. It was in very formal language. He couldn't sign yet, until he had given in his notice at IFS. He folded the sheets neatly and put them back in the envelope.

Time was moving on, but there was no sign of Emma. She was first home each evening, but David really had no idea what time she usually arrived. He made a cup of tea and resorted to watching television. There was nothing on that interested him, so he took his case upstairs and emptied his dirty clothes into the washing basket. As he looked around the bedroom he thought it looked too tidy to have been used recently. When he pulled back the covers his suspicions were confirmed, that the bed had not been slept in. As David came downstairs and inspected the lounge and kitchen-diner, the appearance once more seemed to show that

Emma hadn't been here for a number of days. Where was she then he asked himself? The most obvious person to know would be his daughter, Sue.

'Hello, Sue. Do you know where Mum is?'

'Yes, she's with Pat,' she replied. 'On Friday Pat rang me to say Mum was unwell. She had gone round to have coffee with Mum and she found her slumped in a chair. Pat decided to take Mum to her house. She hasn't eaten much of late. She has a vacant expression on her face. I've been to see her twice over the weekend.'

'Thanks for doing that,' David said. 'But why didn't someone let me know?'

'Mum insisted that we shouldn't bother you. She said you would be busy with meetings and interviews.'

'I was busy, but I would like to have known that she was sick. It doesn't sound good that she's off her food and seems to have lost her sparkle. I'll go and see her and let you know how things are.'

When David arrived at Pat's house, she was full of apologies. 'I'm sorry, I didn't let you know,' she said, 'but that was Emma's wish. My main concern was to do the best for Emma.'

'It's OK,' he said reassuringly. 'I just wondered what had happened knowing she wasn't too well when I went away. I forgot to phone Emma while I was away. I apologise for that.'

'She did say she hadn't heard from you.' As she said this Pat led the way into the sitting room, where Emma was reading. When David entered Emma's face brightened.

'So how are you today?' he asked,

'I'm much better. I can come home with you. I've

got my things ready.'

David thanked Pat for being such a good friend to Emma in her moment of need. His overwhelming gratitude somewhat embarrassed her.

Within a few minutes David and Emma were on their way home. Once there Emma made herself comfortable and continued to read her book. 'I'm going to get myself something to eat,' he said. 'Would you like something?'

'Soup would be nice, with some crusty bread. I'll leave you to choose the flavour.'

'That will be two soups with bread.' David announced rather theatrically. 'Would the lady like tea or coffee?'

'No, water will be fine. And yoghurt would be lovely.'

David heated the vegetable soup and poured it into bowls. He arranged the bread on plates and then made up a tray for Emma and one for himself. He carried Emma's tray through first and then collected his.

'It's lovely to have you back, Darling,' Emma said. He was quite taken aback; he couldn't remember the last time she had called him 'Darling'. 'So how did your trip to Germany go?

'Very well. I had a great time.'

'Wasn't there some mention of a job?' Emma enquired.

'Yes. I have been offered one, starting in a month's time,' David replied.

'So do you want me to go to Germany with you?' This was not the response he had expected. 'I thought it would be good for me to be the wife supporting her husband in his new job.' This was getting more bizarre by the minute. When had Emma ever wanted to help David with his work? She was the career woman who said she never had time to offer him any help!

'There's plenty of time to sort this out before I go,' he said trying to bring closure to this particular conversation. Emma went back to her book, while David cleared the trays into the kitchen. He did a very quick wash of the items they had used for their snack and then went outside to phone Sue. By the time he came back into the house Emma had gone to bed. So much for the wife who was trying to be more supportive and had taken to call him Darling, he thought.

The next morning Emma had got ready and had her breakfast by the time David came downstairs. It looked to him that the improvement in her health was being maintained, on the outside at least. She was smiling and moving about confidently. He knew that problems still existed beneath the surface. Time would tell if these were being resolved or not.

'What are you doing today,' David asked, wondering why Emma was so smartly dressed at such an early hour.

'I have an appointment with Dr Brown to review my medication,' she said. 'Wendy is not at work today, so we're meeting in Tonbridge for coffee. Then I think we'll try some retail therapy. David thought a gentle enquiry about his wife's health was in order.

'How do you feel? You actually look good and you're moving around with poise and confidence.'

'I do feel better than I did a few days ago. I'm not ready to go back to work yet.'

'I'm glad you said that. Seeing you all dressed up,

I thought you were going back before you are ready.'

'Now I wouldn't do that, would I?' Emma exclaimed. 'I'll do what the doctor tells me.' After finishing his coffee, he collected his lunch box and then picked up his brief case from the hall. Almost before he knew it he was on his way to work.

David continued commuting to London each day. His heart was not in his work as it had been before the scandal broke. On his second day back after the German trip, he made an appointment to see Brian. He'd typed an official letter of resignation, to take effect at the end of the month. Brian welcomed him into his office with a handshake. 'How can I help you?' he asked.

David told it as it was. 'You remember how I was shaken by the scandal which hit IFS. I felt I was being blamed in some way.'

Brian was quick to respond. 'I think that was more in your mind than in fact,' he said.

'Be that as it may,' continued David. 'Since that time I have been looking at opportunities that might be available to me. Some firms have taken an interest in me.' David knew this was a lie. Only the Mustermann Corporation had contacted him and subsequently offered him employment, but it sounded good to make out he was being head-hunted. He felt the ground had been prepared and he should now say what he wanted to say with confidence. 'You know I took a few days off, so I could spend a long weekend in Germany. While I was there I was interviewed and offered the position of Director of Finance with a large corporation, which I have accepted.'

'Would that be the Mustermann Corporation?'

Brian asked.

David winced. 'You know about this corporation?' he asked.

'Let's say the paths of IFS and the Mustermann Corporation have crossed from time to time. We have done business. We have helped them and they have helped us,' Brian said. David felt his opportunity to emerge victorious from this meeting had all but disappeared. It was Brian who held the trump hand, with his revelation about IFS and the Mustermann Corporation working together. That begged so many questions, questions that David couldn't bring himself to ask Brian. It was time to retire gracefully without being put down any further.

'I have written a letter of resignation,' he said, as he handed Brian the envelope. 'I hope I can be released from my contract with IFS at the end of the month, so I am free to start work with the Mustermann Corporation sometime in early October.' Brian didn't open the envelope. He merely thanked David for it and hoped he would be happy in his new post.

David received a letter from the CEO at International Financial Services, acknowledging his letter of resignation. He thanked David for his work at IFS and wished him well for the future. Now there was nothing to stop David from writing to Herr Mustermann, accepting the post of Director of Finance on the agreed terms and salary. He confirmed that he would start work on Monday 6th October. He heard nothing more from Klaus Mustermann. More surprising perhaps was that David had heard nothing from Anna. He knew she was very busy, finishing one job and starting another. After their parting at Stuttgart airport he had the right to be concerned. It would have taken her only a few minutes to get in touch, he thought.

After several more days of frustration, David took the initiative and sent a text to Anna. 'Know U R busy. How R things going? xD' In less than an hour she rang him. 'Hello, David. I have completed my work for the Mustermanns. I am now preparing to start work in London.'

'So where are you?'

'In London.'

David wasted no time. 'See you for a meal at our restaurant, seven o'clock tomorrow.'

'I look forward to it. See you then.' With that Anna ended the call.

That night when David arrived home Emma had preparations for the evening meal well in hand. 'It is good that you're home early tonight, so we can eat together,' she said.

'Yes, but it won't be like that every night,' he replied. 'Tomorrow I'll be home late. Lots to clear away before I leave IFS. Time's getting short.'

'I know,' Emma said, 'but it is so nice to be together.'

After washing his hands, David poured himself some wine from the bottle on the work surface. Emma followed him flirtatiously. He moved to look for some peanuts to eat as he enjoyed his wine. As he was pondering his next move, the timer on the cooker saved him from being pursued any further. This was a worrying development on Emma's part, he thought.

Anna arrived at the restaurant a few minutes before David. She pulled him towards her as they kissed.

'How are you?' he asked.

'I'm well.'

'So what are you doing at the moment?'

'I am doing some induction, shadowing Shirley, an established member of staff,' Anna said.

'What are you intending to do in the short term?'

'Return to Germany.'

'What?' David was surprised at Anna's apparent change of plans. 'A few weeks ago you couldn't get to London quickly enough to get yourself a job. Now you intend going back to Germany. Why the change?'

'You getting a job with the Mustermanns has changed everything. I want to be there when you are there!' she explained with a twinkle in her eye.

'Are things still on then?' he asked.

'Of course. They have never been off as far as I am concerned.'

'So what was going on during my weekend in Stuttgart?' he asked.

'Things were against us. I was given lots to keep me busy.'

'That was a bit unfair,' David said. 'Do the parents suspect then?'

'Perhaps they have picked up a few clues. Franz has probably kept them up to date with developments.'

'Why are they being so protective? After all you are forty.'

Anna explained. 'You have to see it from their point of view. I am forty, but they are the ones who took me in and gave me a home. They feel responsible. They do not want to see me hurt.'

David continued to ask searching questions. 'Will

you ever be completely free?'

'Of course. I am no longer employed by the Mustermann Corporation. You will replace me soon. That will not be reversed. Soon I will be encouraged to leave home too.' Anna's words and body language set his mind at rest. He now had to be patient and wait for her words to come true. So he changed the subject. He asked about the domestic arrangements when he went to live in Stuttgart.

'You will probably be accommodated in the castle for a few days. Then in a small hotel,' Anna said. 'There are a few hotels that have links with the Mustermanns.' This was reassuring news to David. They continued to talk about their respective new jobs during the meal. Then David thought he should tell Anna about things at home.

'Emma, my wife, has a responsible job with the health service in the UK. Since she returned to work after our holiday in France she has found the pressure too much. At present she is off sick.'

'I am sorry to hear about that. From things you have said in the past, I realised all was not well.'

'Recently she has been acting like the adoring wife. When I'm away, such as when I went to Stuttgart, she goes to pieces. When I return, she's back to normal.'

'You do have a problem,' Anna said.

'When I told her about my new job in Germany, she said she would go there to be with me and offer support.' Anna screwed up her face, but said nothing. 'I will have to work something out soon,' he said.

Anna looked at her watch and said, 'I must be off. Things to do.'

'OK, I'll pay,' David said.

'I think it unlikely that I will see you before you go to Stuttgart next month,' she said. 'There are just so many things to do.' David nodded in agreement.

'We can keep in touch by mobile,' he said.

Anna said, 'That would be good.' She stood up and moved round the table to David. As she came near she put her arms around his neck, pulling him closer. They engaged in a brief, but passionate, kiss.

'I'll see you then,' he said. He hoped it wouldn't be too long.

During this time Emma's health continued to improve and she seemed to be enjoying life again. She got herself more involved in the social life of the village, joining the WI and an art and craft club. However these were not without their problems. Sadly she felt tolerated rather than accepted. She tried to arrive early for meetings, so she didn't have to join an existing group. Then as people arrived they formed their own groups and left Emma on her own. She did manage to make friends with some of the younger and newer residents of Penshurst. The older and long-time residents were the ones who gave her a hard time. This was yet another difficulty about which Emma would have to give some serious thought.

17

THE CURTAIN FALLS

During the days that followed, David's life was in constant turmoil. Not only was he changing jobs, but his new post was overseas. Packing was one of his biggest nightmares. He put things in the spare room ready to be packed. Emma usually did this, for which he was very grateful. This time he was on his own.

David invited all those in his team at IFS to go out for a meal with him. They were happy to do so and they had a good time. At the end of the meal there was a presentation to David and a bunch of flowers for Emma. Among his gifts was a pocket-size English-German dictionary. He thanked them for their gifts. He went on to say how much he appreciated their hard work and support over the years. Someone commented that it was a pity David had turned down the chance of having an official IFS send-off. David replied that he had no recollection of ever having been offered one.

Emma was getting more and more worked up about David's departure. She continued to fuss around him like a mother hen. When he needed space she was there to fill it. He made an appointment to see Dr Brown, to review Emma's state of health and her medication. David described Emma's present state. 'Her personality has changed markedly of late,' he said. 'She has become more adoring and clingy. It's nice to feel wanted, but she is overdoing it. While I'm away she goes rapidly downhill physically and psychologically. When I return, she picks up again.'

'She is looking to you for support at the moment,' suggested Dr Brown. 'Whereas in the past, she would have been able to cope perfectly well on her own.' David nodded. 'Does she still take her tablets when you are away?'

'I can't be sure,' David said. 'There are no tablets about the house. That's something I need to ask her friends and my daughter to keep an eye on while I'm away.'

David had invited 'the boys' to a farewell party at the Chafford Arms that night. He had asked Emma if she wanted to come with him, but she had declined, saying, 'I don't want to spend a night at the Chafford Arms with a lot of blokes.'

It was a friendly and lively occasion. There was plenty of humour and back-slapping. Story tellers were in their element. David bought the first round of drinks and another round later on. The landlord proposed a toast to David, for having the guts to step out into the unknown. One of the ladies raised a glass to Emma for putting up with David for so long!

The next day was Saturday and David, Sue and Steve had planned to meet up in Penshurst for a family get-together to say their farewells. It would also give them the chance to check the plans for looking after Emma while David was away. David had also asked a number of Emma's friends to join them. The day went well. As people left there were handshakes, hugs and kisses for David and for Emma too. People realised it was going to be harder for her than for him. Members of the family helped to clear up and load and re-load the dishwasher. Then they took their leave. Nobody knew what to say as they left, uncertain of what the future held in store.

That night David experienced his dream again. As last time, there were bodies strewn across the cobbled street. As he walked amongst them he again recognised the faces of people he knew well. Their faces and hands were raised to the sky pleadingly. He walked beyond the corpses and he could see a soldier crouched behind a machine gun. As he moved closer, he could identify the soldier responsible for the killings. He had seen that face before, adorning some of the walls in the castle. It was as if it had been cut from the black and white photo and stuck on the machine gunner. It was the original Max Mustermann. What should he do? He had thrown in his lot with the Mustermanns. There was no going back. David woke up shrieking loudly and he woke Emma.

'What's the matter?' she cried. David was sweating profusely and his body was shaking uncontrollably. Amidst his sobs, he managed to explain what had happened in his dream.

'It was my friends that were shot,' he managed to say. 'I know who did it. I recognised him.' Emma had never seen David in such a state before. She felt powerless to do anything. She came and stood beside him as he sat on the edge of the bed. Slowly the convulsions died down and the sobbing stopped. He looked and felt like a miserable wretch. He went down the stairs slowly and Emma followed at a distance. He lowered himself gently onto a chair and managed to speak, 'Fine preparation for starting a job in Germany in a week's time,' he said.

'You sit and take it easy,' Emma said. 'I'll make a cup of tea.' Gradually David returned to normal. He took himself off to have a shower and get dressed. This experience had left an indelible scar on his soul.

Steve had agreed to take his father to Gatwick. He arranged to stay the night before, so they could make an early start the next morning. Emma was up and dressed early. Her face was drawn and she looked agitated.

'Have you taken your tablets, Mum?' Steve asked.

'Yes, I take them every day with my breakfast.'

'Are you coming to Gatwick to see Dad off?' 'No, I don't think so. I'll say my farewells here.'

Steve put David's case in the boot, together with his shoulder bag and laptop. Emma and David were alone together for just a few moments. Each struggled to find the right words to say. It was an agonising farewell.

'I do hope things work out well,' Emma said.

'Yes, so do I,' David answered. 'I will try and phone you each day. You have lots of friends to help you.'

'I know,' she said. They hugged each other and David realised this was the closest he had been to Emma for a long time. Although she held him tightly, he could see from the look on her face that her mind was far away. As the car moved down the drive David looked back and saw Emma's face behind the net curtains. Tears filled his eyes.

It was a pleasant flight to Stuttgart. David had sent Anna a text to say what time he would arrive. Franz was there to meet him. 'What are you doing for lunch?' Franz asked. Without waiting for a reply he said, 'I can put a few things together if that's OK.'

'Fine,' said David.

During lunch Franz discussed the finances of the Mustermann Corporation with David. Afterwards he switched on a computer and explained the layout of the spreadsheets and then he left so David could investigate further. Over the next few days he did more searches. He was amazed, not only by the number of transactions, but also by the names of businesses with which the Corporation traded.

David surprised himself that he remembered to phone Emma every day during the first few days he was away. She sounded fine. He was concerned that she again spoke about coming to be with him in Germany. David soon realised he needed a car. He felt isolated. He longed to go into Stuttgart, but he knew that was out of the question. He made a mental note to bring his Mondeo the next time he travelled back from the UK. As the days went by, David felt more confident in the work he was doing, but he did feel extremely lonely. He missed working in a team. There was so much conversation and banter between those in his department at IFS, but here he felt isolated. He missed a night out with his mates at the Chafford Arms. Since he had been in Stuttgart he had heard nothing from Anna. He sent her a text, 'How R things with you? Job going well - outside of work I'm bored & lonely. When am I going 2 C U? Dx'

Anna replied later that day, 'I am coming 2 Stutt soon. Then things will B better 4 both of us xA'

The next day David was working on some particularly long lists of transactions with a pharmaceutical company. He had checked all the figures twice and obtained a different result each time. On the third attempt his mobile rang, but he ignored it to keep himself completely focussed on the job in hand. Later his phone rang again and he answered it.

'Hello, it's Sue. Mum's dead!' Mobiles sometimes lose signal and at times the voice becomes distorted or inaudible, but this message was crystal clear. His heart quickened, his gut tightened and his mind turned somersaults.

'How? When? Where?' David cried out.

'This morning Pat went round to see if she was OK. Mum was dead in bed.'

'Oh, I don't know what to say. I'll fly home later today. I'll let you know times. Can someone pick me up at Gatwick?'

'Of course,' Sue said. 'Pat dialled 999. Police, ambulance, Dr Brown arrived. It was harrowing for him. He had to certify Mum was dead. She's been taken away for a post-mortem.'

'How terrible for the doctor. He's been helping your Mum to get back to work. They worked together at the Health Centre.'

The ever-efficient Sue suggested she, David and Steve should meet up that evening to make plans for the funeral. She had contacted the undertaker, leaving a message with the receptionist that her mother had died.

'I'll see you later,' he said, trying to hold back the tears. He closed down all the applications he had open.

Then he rang Franz.

'You must go home as soon as you can,' Franz said. 'I will book your airline tickets.'

'Make it a single to Gatwick,' David said, 'I will travel by car when I return.'

David was in a complete daze on the flight to Gatwick. His wife and faithful companion for twenty-eight years had been taken from him. He would never see her alive again. Things hadn't been good between them over these past few months. Their relationship had been bumping along. But he would no longer have her there to ask for advice, to criticise him, to encourage him, to keep his feet on the ground. Tears filled his eyes as he thought of the impact Emma's death would have on his daughter, Sue, and her husband, Tom, and their dear children. These little ones would never again be able to cuddle and kiss grandma. Never again would they enjoy grandma's cooking and show her what they had done at school. Steve and Jo would take it stoically, but Emma's death would still shake them. Little Fiona was too young to know what had happened. Emma's friends would be overcome with grief. She was the first of the girls to die. They had been strong and encouraging during her illness, but how would they react to her death? What about all those who worked at the Health Centre? What impact would Emma's death have on them? They constantly had to get alongside grieving relations or parents, but how would they cope when it was one of their own? Who had let Emma down? Dr. Brown? No, he was trying to encourage her back to full health so she could return to work. The family had encouraged and supported Emma.

What about me? David thought. How much have I

contributed to Emma's death? He and Emma never saw eye-to-eye on many things. She always seemed to say the opposite of what he said. His meeting up with Anna in Normandy and since had rubbed salt into the wounds of their marriage. But Anna was fun to be with, witty and clever. Should he have stopped seeing her after that first chance meeting in Carentan? It may have been better for Emma if he had seen Anna no more. But what about his life? He would surely have gone downhill because of the scandal at IFS and Emma's deteriorating health. Was he right or wrong to do what he'd done? But all of this was now in the past. As he had told Emma, the past is gone and you can't do anything about it. Nothing or nobody could undo what had happened. He could only live in the present and look to the future. At that moment the Captain spoke to say they would take a bit longer to fly into Gatwick, as he was circum-navigating a thunderstorm! As the plane touched down and taxied towards the terminal, David was thankful for a safe landing. He walked through the arrivals hall and met up with Steve.

'Terrible business,' Steve said. 'Can't believe I brought you here just a few days ago.'

'How has Jo taken it?' David asked.

'Shocked like the rest of us.'

'You're staying at the cottage tonight?'

'Yes, but I need to be off home early tomorrow morning,' Steve said.

Steve pulled into the drive. As he did so, Sue opened the front door and ran out to meet her father and brother. They all found it difficult to keep back the tears. In silence the three of them held on to each other, demonstrating their unity in grief.

'We've got to be strong for each other and our families,' David said. 'How I wish this had never happened. It's times like this when you experience the strength of the family.'

'We'll support each other,' said Sue. 'We've done so in the past and we'll do it again. I've made a casserole for our meal. After that we can sort out what needs to be done while we have coffee.

Sue told Steve she had contacted the undertaker soon after hearing about her mother's death. 'There will have to be an inquest because Mum's death was unexplained,' she said. 'But there's no reason why we shouldn't plan the funeral. It's booked for a week on Wednesday at Tonbridge Wells Crematorium at 2pm.'

'What do we do about flowers?' David asked. 'Do we go for one floral display from all the family?'

'I think Jo will want one from us,' said Steve. 'You will probably want to do the same,' he said looking at Sue.

'Yes. Then there could be a separate one from you, Dad,' she said.

'What shall we do about other flowers?' David asked. 'Family flowers only?'

'I don't think you can do that,' said Sue. 'Mum had a lot of friends. They would be so upset if we said they couldn't send a floral tribute for Mum. Then there's everyone at the Health Centre.'

'OK,' said David. 'So we encourage people to send flowers. Then we distribute them to appropriate places after the funeral. Agreed?' Steve and Sue nodded.

'We do need to put something in the paper,' said

Steve, 'to tell people Mum has died and give details of the funeral.' The others agreed. Steve said he would draft something and email it to David and Sue for comments before he sent it to the paper.

'We also need an obituary,' said Sue. 'You're the best person to do that, Dad.'

'I'll do it, but I need some information from you two and her friends,' David said.

Sue said she would contact the undertaker as soon as possible and arrange a meeting between him and the three of them, to make arrangements for the funeral. David agreed to go to the Registry Office as soon as he was told that the post-mortem had been completed and the green form was available.

David then shared an idea that he'd had. 'I thought it would be good to have an open house at the Chafford Arms after the funeral. 'It would give friends and family a chance to gather together in memory of Mum.' Sue and Steve were in favour of the idea. David agreed to arrange this. He also said he would start making enquiries through his solicitor about what legal procedures needed to be addressed.

'It's things like surrendering Mum's passport and National Insurance number,' said Sue. 'I only found out today that we have to do this.'

'All the sorting out of her personal items can wait until after the funeral,' David said.

After several hours, with interruptions for coffee and phone calls, David, Sue and Steve felt they had done all they could.

Over the following days David and his children completed the tasks they had set themselves. Some of the most difficult and harrowing experiences for

David were receiving cards and phone calls expressing sympathy. Worse still was meeting people face to face. There was an endless stream of callers to the cottage. Each had to be welcomed, given a drink and the opportunity to talk about Emma. Meeting people in the street was even more challenging. At times David was reduced to tears by what people said about Emma and the difference she had made to so many people's lives. He was now beginning to understand what it had been like for Emma to experience the staring eyes and gossip resulting from newspaper reports about their holiday in Normandy. At times David just wanted to get away and hide. He would go home for a rest, intending to resume his visits in town sometime later. Once he reached home he had more visitors and phone calls to attend to. He was fast reaching the stage of being unable to cope.

One of those who telephoned was Dr. Brown, his GP. 'I'm terribly sad to hear of your wife's passing,' he said.

'Thank you. It's been a big shock to us all,' David replied. Dr. Brown arranged to call in and see David that same day.

'I thought you would rather I came to you than you having to come to the surgery,' the doctor said on his arrival. 'I now have the results of the post-mortem. These show that Mrs Burrows died of natural causes. There were no traces of foreign substances in her body, which she may have taken, or which may have been given to her by someone else.'

'That's a relief,' said David. 'I got the impression that everything was just too much for her; the extra pressure at work; my suspension from IFS; publicity from our holiday; my new job in Germany. Emma just opted out.'

'It's happened to others,' said Dr. Brown. He declined the offer of a cup of tea. He stood up and once again expressed his heartfelt sympathy.

The meeting with the undertaker, Philip Cripps, went satisfactorily. Steve, Sue and David admitted afterwards that the most difficult discussion was over the coffin. David pointed out that it was not intended to last, so there was no point in spending a fortune on it. Two hymns were chosen, The Lord's my shepherd and All things bright and beautiful. Mr Cripps said Rev. Dolman, who lived near the crematorium, would take the funeral service.

'He would appreciate something in writing about Mrs Burrows' life,' Mr Cripps said. 'You could get it to the office, or I could collect it.' David, Sue and Steve agreed to pass something on to him in the next few days.

David booked up the Chafford Arms for a buffet after the service at the crematorium. He told Sue and Steve, 'I'll pay whatever it costs. I want it to be a really good do for people to remember your Mum. No curled up sandwiches and dry cake. Let's do it properly. 'I'll pay for everyone's first drink.'

18

GOODBYE

The day of the funeral was grey and miserable. Far more people came along than could be seated in the crematorium chapel. Many stood at the back and many more outside. The singing of the hymns matched the dismal day. Perhaps some people were affected by the occasion, while others were not used to singing hymns. Whatever the reason, the hymn singing left much to be desired. After the service, people filed out and looked at the mass of floral tributes in silence. Then they got into their cars where they were no longer on show and they made their way to the Chafford Arms. There the get-together lived up to what David in particular had hoped for. Friends chatted with friends and those they had never met before. There was a great atmosphere, as people came to remember not only Emma but also to speak to David and his family.

David stood up and the landlord rang the bell to get people's attention. 'First of all I want to thank you for coming to the crematorium and coming on here,'

David said. 'Thank you for all your help and support since Emma passed away. Thank you for the flowers, letters, cards, phone calls and visits, expressing your love and concern. I thank you and I speak on behalf of Sue and Tom, Steve and Jo, in expressing our heartfelt thanks to each one of you. Thanks to Terry and his staff, for making the Chafford Arms available, and for laying on such a splendid spread.'

'As you can imagine, it hasn't been easy over the past week or so. Today's service at the crematorium was not an easy experience. The vicar did his best. Sue, Steve and I had given him some information about Emma to be used in the service. He didn't know her. As I heard him speaking, I thought, he's got an impossible task. How can you do justice to a person who has led a full and active life in just a few minutes? How can you say something worthwhile about Emma, who was wife, mother, grandma, friend and Health Centre manager? The answer is you can't. My hope is that all the memories we have of Emma from the past will sustain us in the present and help us in the future.'

'As you know, I have only recently started a new job in Germany. I will be going back to resume work sometime next week. I will be keeping the cottage on, at least for now, so I have somewhere in the UK that I can call home. Thanks once again for all you have done. I hope our paths will continue to cross in the years ahead.' Applause rang out across the pub as David sat down.

David busied himself in sorting out Emma's estate during the days that followed. The family had arranged to come to the cottage the weekend after the funeral. They arrived on Friday evening. After a meal and putting the children to bed, David, his children and their spouses set about making plans for what had to be done.

'I've briefed Will Howlett, our solicitor,' said David. 'He's a good man. He will keep me up to date. I'm not thinking of making a hasty decision to sell the cottage,' he continued. 'Nobody knows how this job in Germany will work out. I need time to let the dust settle.'

'Who's going to take care of this place?' asked Steve.

'I've met with some of Mum's friends,' said Sue. 'They've agreed to get the post in and give it a clean from time to time. I'll leave them to sort that out. I'll keep in contact with them and ask them to let me know if there's anything they're concerned about.'

'We must keep in touch,' David said. 'We've always been close as a family and we need to support each other through these difficult days and keep each other abreast of the latest developments with regard to mum's affairs.'

When David left the room, Sue and Tom, Steve and Jo had a brief discussion about disposing of Emma's clothes. 'Once Dad has gone to Germany, Sue said, 'Jo and I can pop over and start sorting the clothes. I know mum had a few watches, bracelets and pendants, but I'm not sure what else we might find.'

David re-appeared with a tray of drinks. Sue felt she had to bring up the matter of her mum's possessions with him. 'Dad, Jo and I will come over sometime and sort through mum's clothes.'

'I would appreciate that,' said David.

'But what about the many personal things,' Sue continued. 'They are personal to you too,' she said looking at her dad.

'Why don't we go and collect the drawers from the dressing table and chest of drawers and bring them in here?' asked David. 'Then we can see how much there is and make a start on sorting it.'

They went backwards and forwards to the bedroom until all the drawers were brought downstairs. The larger ones contained sheets and pillow slips, jumpers and blouses and Sue put these aside to attend to later. The more interesting finds were in the smaller drawers, which contained tights, gloves and pieces of jewellery. At the bottom there were photos, letters, post-cards and miscellaneous bills going back over a number of years. There were also three official-looking enve-lopes, which had been opened very meticulously with a letter opener or knife.

'Who's this then?' asked Tom, as he and Sue examined one of the photos. Tom held it up so everyone could see. It showed Emma arm-in-arm with a young man. 'It's certainly not you, David,' Tom remarked.

'I don't recognise him,' David said, as he scru-tinised the photo. He turned it over, hoping to find a clue about the man's identity. On the back was the date 1985. 'That was after we were engaged,' David said angrily.

'Are you sure you want to do this?' Sue asked her father. 'There could be more embarrassing revelations.'

'It's got to be done, embarrassing or not,' he said.

The next item David found was a postcard from the Lake District sent to Emma Simmonds, which was her maiden name. 'Dear Emma,' David read. 'Thought you would like to see the beauty of the countryside we are walking through. John.'

'When's the postmark?' asked Steve.

'June 1984. The actual date is smudged,' said David, 'At least that was before we were engaged.'

'So do we think that John is the one in the photo with mum?' Sue asked.

'I don't know, David said. 'She never spoke about going out with anyone before she met me. In fact I know nothing of her life before we met.'

'You make it sound rather melodramatic,' Tom said.

As they continued to sort through the drawers, they came across more photos. Some were in black and white, others in sepia. A number of them depicted older people in formal dress. The family deduced these were probably Emma's grandparents or their generation. Some of the sepia photos were in card frames, with the name of the photographer clearly displayed on the reverse, but no clues about the people in the photograph. There were no photographs of Emma when she was young and none depicting her parents labelled as such. David told them that the first occasion when he had asked Emma about her parents, all she would say was, 'I don't have any.' David had taken that to mean they were dead. He and Emma had rarely spoken about their childhood memories. He came to realise that her response probably meant that she never knew her parents. Her early life was a closed book and she was reluctant to open it and disclose its contents, even to her husband. In her passport her place of birth was given as Sheffield. David had never seen Emma's birth certificate. It was as if the early part of her life didn't exist. After looking through several more photographs of people nobody recognised, David suggested they call a halt. 'I think we've spent enough time on these,' he said. 'There's another day tomorrow.'

The next morning they continued examining the contents of the drawers left over from the previous night. David was intrigued by the three envelopes. He looked at the postmarks very carefully and removed the contents of the most recent one, postmarked March 2014. He unfolded the sheets and spread them on the table. After a pause he said, 'Well I'm blowed!' It was a bank statement for an Easy Saver account in the name of Emma Burrows. David's eyes ran quickly down the columns of the two sheets to the balance at the end of the second sheet. 'Look at this,' he exclaimed. '£36,063 in an account of your mum's which I knew nothing about!'

'How did mum get £36,000?' asked Sue. 'And how come she never told you?'

'I don't know,' answered David. 'I don't think we're going to find an answer to that today. That will be something to take up with the solicitor and bank.' The remaining envelopes contained bank statements for Emma's Easy Saver account for the previous two years. The balance had remained more or less the same. David felt fortunate to have his family with him at a time like this. He and Emma had brought their children up to help and support each other and it was good to see they were bringing up their children in the same caring way. Sue and Jo managed to divide up Emma's jewellery between them, without any disagreement. Any items they thought they would never wear, they agreed to offer to Emma's friends. When the box containing Emma's engagement ring was opened, Jo said to Sue,

'You should have that.'

Steve asked, 'Why was it in the box and not on her finger?'

'She didn't want to damage it or lose it,' said David. 'She hardly ever wore it.'

'Seems a pity,' said Steve. 'It's such an exquisite ring.'

David said nothing to the others concerning the revelations about Emma's life before she was married and the discovery of her secret bank account. These had somewhat shaken his confidence and trust in his deceased wife. He made an appointment to see his solicitor at the earliest opportunity.

After the customary handshake, David got straight down to business.

'Last week I and my family sorted out a lot of Emma's personal items. We came across a photo of Emma with another man and correspondence from 'John', possibly the same man, sent from the Lake District. We also discovered Emma had a secret bank account.' Mr. Howlett locked his hands tightly together, as if he was in some strange attitude of prayer. He looked at David and smiled.

'With regards to the former dilemma you presented to me,' he said, 'you will understand there is nothing I can do. The death of Mrs Burrows will have broken any relationship that existed. Her marriage to you and a relationship with anyone else have ended with her passing, even if the other person is still alive. It remains to be seen if Mrs Burrows has left any legal document in favour of another person, outside yourself and your family. I have looked out the will that you and Mrs Burrows made in 2005. This is very clear. When one of you dies, in this case Mrs Burrows, the estate passes to the surviving partner. This means you inherit Mrs Burrows' estate. If Mrs Burrows has made any changes to that will in favour of another, she has not involved me in drawing up the changes and producing a certified will. Time will tell if any claimant emerges.' This last statement caused David considerable concern over the fate of Emma's estate.

Will Howlett continued, 'Over the matter of Mrs Burrows' bank account you knew nothing about, you will have to take this up with the bank.' As David left the solicitor's office he felt reassured that he would inherit all that he and Emma had held jointly, but he felt more uneasy about Emma's secret bank account.

The bank cashier expressed her deepest sympathy over Emma's death. David explained about the bank account that existed in his wife's name and about which none of the family had any knowledge.

'Do you have details of the account?' she asked. David pushed the Statement for March 2014 to the cashier. She confirmed she had found the account. 'I can't do anything further today. I could make an appointment for you to see Les Simpkins, the Assistant Manager, later in the week. He will be able to sort this out for you,' she said. David agreed to return on Thursday at 11am.

Every time David went out he would meet friends he hadn't seen since Emma passed away. Men exchanged handshakes and ladies kisses and all expressed sympathy and sadness at his sad loss. He hadn't heard from Anna recently, so he sent a text to warn her of his impending departure from England. Anna sent an immediate reply, saying the Mustermann family was looking forward to him returning to his job in Germany. Reading between the lines David assumed that she had been filling in for him in Stuttgart. She said she was eagerly awaiting his return.

David's appointment at the bank confirmed Emma's account contained £36,063. 'It has maintained roughly that balance over a number of years,' said the Assistant Manager.

'Do you know when it was opened?' David asked.

'In May 1989,' Mr Simpkins replied. 'Is there any way your wife could have come into a large sum of money at this time, or months, perhaps years, before this?'

'Nothing I can think of.'

'All I can say is that after the account was opened in May 1989, there have been no payments into the account or withdrawals from it. The only change has been the addition of a small amount of interest each year. This has been at a more beneficial rate in the past than is the case today.'

David thanked Mr Simpkins for the information he had presented. 'As I'm the sole beneficiary of my wife's estate, the money in this account will presumably come to me,' he said.

'Yes, unless there is a will to the contrary. We can transfer that money to your account when Mrs. Burrows' estate is finally wound up,' said Mr. Simpkins. Both men stood up and shook hands and the Assistant Manager opened his office door so David could leave.

During the days that followed David was occupied with clearing up the cottage, working out how much luggage he could fit in the Mondeo and thinking about his new life in Germany. His moods swung from excitement to panic, from being self-assured, to wondering if this was going to be a ghastly mistake. The family had arranged to go to the cottage for lunch on the Sunday before he was due to leave. 'Jo and I will do the cooking,' Sue had said. A few days before, David had a phone call from his daughter.

'Daddy, Steve and I have had a letter from a firm of solicitors in London. I knew Steve wouldn't ring, so I rang him and now I'm phoning you. The letter says that according to the will of Mrs. Emma Burrows, deceased, I stand to inherit just over £18,000 from Mum's estate.'

'What?' exclaimed David. 'I thought £36,000 was coming to me. I've no objection to it going to you and Steve; it will all go to you when I die.'

'We'll bring the letters and talk about this on Sunday,' Sue said. 'Bye for now.' She realised this latest piece of news had unsettled her dad. A telephone conversation was no way to sort this out amicably, hence the abrupt end to her call.

David was astonished by this turn of events. Not only did Emma have a secret bank account, but also she had made a separate will, bequeathing the money in her account to Sue and Steve. It wasn't the fact that he wouldn't automatically inherit the money along with the rest of her estate that annoyed him, but that Emma had so obviously decided the money would never be his. This raised more questions about where the money came from and why she had kept the account secret. Anna continued to send encouraging texts to David, saying how much she was looking forward to seeing him again.

David was determined to give his family a loving welcome when they arrived for lunch on Sunday and he managed to do this. He was keen to maintain the good relationship that existed between them. 'I know everything will go to you in the future,' he said, looking at Sue and Steve, 'but I thought it would be transferred to me in the meantime.' When I spoke to the Assistant Manager in the bank, he agreed that I would inherit Mum's separate bank account, unless there is a will to the contrary. Did he know something?' David and his family examined the contents of the solicitor's letters over drinks before lunch. Both letters indicated that payments would be sent out in due course, on the winding up of Emma's estate. In the meantime Sue and Steve were requested to reply confirming their identity. David pointed out to them what was written at the bottom of each letter, namely that expenses for further correspondence and telephone calls would be charged at the rate of £300 per hour.

'Keep it brief,' said David, 'otherwise you lose part of your inheritance!'

It was a good final get-together over lunch. 'When are you leaving?' asked Tom.

'Tomorrow morning,' said David. 'I've booked the shuttle.'

'It should be exciting,' Steve said. 'A new start; well almost!'

'I'm looking forward to it. I'll take my time travelling to Stuttgart. Perhaps take two or three days to get there. I'll try and stop in Luxemburg; I've never been there before. There are places in France and Germany along the way that I've not visited either. This is my chance.'

'Sounds like some holiday,' Sue said.

'Don't forget you'll all be welcome to come and see me. Perhaps at Christmas, if I'm still there,' David said.

As they said their farewells, some of the most telling words came from Rachel. 'We miss Grandma, now we're going to miss you too, Grandad.'

'But it's only for a short time,' David said, trying to prevent the tears welling up in his eyes.

The next morning David was up early. He went and left a key with Pat. They embraced and wished each other all the best for the future. He managed to fit into the car everything he had packed. His golf clubs could be taken later if he needed them. He enjoyed his trip across part of Europe. He visited some beautiful places and met some interesting people. Every day he received encouraging texts from Anna. On day three her text read, 'I'll C U in Castle Park. Let me know eta.'

At last David made it and within an hour of the time he had told Anna. 'Mission accomplished,' he said as he embraced Anna and gave her a passionate kiss.

'Let's go for a drink,' she said; 'I have so much to tell you.' Her excitement of recent days was increasing by the minute. 'Klaus has rented a flat for us. He now considers we are one. The money for the rent will be taken from your salary.'

'How do you feel about these arrangements?'

Anna grasped his arm and said, 'I'm ecstatic!' She continued telling David the good news; 'I have a job with a bank in Stuttgart. It has links with IFS in the UK. Isn't that good?'

David gave Anna a smile that turned into a huge grin. 'It's fantastic; all so unbelievable,' he said. 'Can we go to the flat to unload my car? Then I can have a shower before we go out for a meal.'

'Sounds good, but who's paying?' she asked.

'I'd like to pay, but I haven't got any euros!' he replied.

Once at the flat, David couldn't help noticing that Anna had been very busy.

'You've made this place look good; it's very welcoming,' he said.

'I have been here for three days, so it would be ready for your arrival.'

After a sumptuous meal in Stuttgart, David and Anna returned to the flat. She had already prepared the bed and she wasn't slow to get into it. David quickly followed her.

'I've been waiting for this moment for a long time,' David said.

'Me too,' said Anna. 'At last I can be myself!'

ABOUT THE AUTHOR

Derek Ames, a retired science teacher from Onehouse in Suffolk, has self- published 'Encounters'. It is written under the pen name of Drake Mees and was inspired by some bizarre happenings that took place during a holiday in Normandy in August 2013, particularly involving fishermen. It is a novel, but based on real places.

Derek began to write as soon as he returned home. "I enjoyed developing the story that came to me on holiday," he said. "I wrote for two or three hours for several nights each week and it was fascinating how the storyline just flowed." Although he had never attempted writing a book before, Derek enjoyed the experience, with encouragement and help from family and friends. 'Encounters' took about eighteen months to write.

If you had suggested a few years ago that Derek would write and publish a book he would have said it was very unlikely. "I have an optimistic attitude to life, and I believe it's possible to do things that most people won't attempt. However, I would not have put writing and publishing a book near the top of my list of things to do!".

THE SEQUEL

By the end of the story so many questions remain unanswered and demand a sequel. 'An Encounter Too Far' also written by Drake Mees, should provide some answers about David and Anna's past and what happens to them in their life together. It is due for publication sometime in 2020.

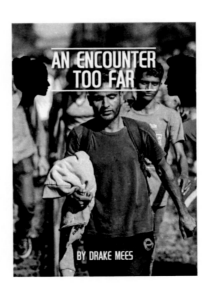